July 2002

To Jan and K

Following o
at Chaos Magna,
Warwick,

Maxine

GW01403394

A BROWN BIRD SINGING

Maxine Davies

MINERVA PRESS
LONDON
ATLANTA MONTREUX SYDNEY

ISBN 0 75410 010 3

First Published 1998 by
MINERVA PRESS
195 Knightsbridge
London SW7 1RE

Printed in Great Britain for Minerva Press

A BROWN BIRD SINGING

*To
my family
and
Stef Pixner*

Throughout this book surnames have been used except where confidentiality is appropriate, or when I cannot recall a surname.

About the Author

Born in Bristol, I lived in London for forty years. I love the infinite diversity and cosmopolitan ambience of the city.

I am single, have three goddaughters and five nieces and nephews. My interests include music, playing the recorder, reading autobiographies, gardening, walking in and around Bristol, and my three cats. I enjoy visiting historic and beautiful places. Having kept a journal since I was fifteen, I have written letters, poems and articles printed in a wide range of publications. This is my first book.

My secondary education was at Marist Convent, Fulham. Initially I worked as an au pair in Paris, then as a bookings clerk for the Ramblers' Association and Wings Travel Agency, enjoying travel abroad. Later I worked in Malta, and Philadelphia, USA.

After training as a social worker at the University of Bristol, I worked in childcare and medical social work in Wandsworth. Returning to Avon in 1975 I specialised in adoption and fostering.

Seeking wider experience I joined the ILEA/GLC for seven years, working in colleges, personnel and the Women's Committee Support Unit, then as a staff welfare officer.

During the 1980s I trained in gestalt therapy at the Pellin Centre, working as a therapist with women, also as a generic social worker and tutor in journal writing for Kensington and Chelsea.

In 1992 I returned to Bristol, working freelance as a counsellor, group facilitator and tutor of journal writing.

I now have plenty of time to write and have begun a sequel to this book, *London Calling*.

Acknowledgements

Reece Winstone – Bristol in the 1940s.

Yesterday's Bristol – Newspaper for information on the war including the buddleia which flourished afterwards.

Offbeat Bristol – James Belsey for the story of Nipper the Dog.

The Rose was sung by Bette Midler in the film *The Rose*.

Own writing previously published.

Dream On – Bristol Writers on Cinema – piece on Saturday morning Cinema 1994.

Journal of Bristol and Avon Family History Society – Article on James White, December 1994.

Special Thanks To

Stef Pixner psychotherapist in London for bread, strife and roses.

Clare Roberts at the Gerda Boyessen Centre, Acton, London for touch which released memories.

Penny Thomas psychotherapist in Bristol for being there while I wrote my way through the past, and more.

Jenny Emmerson who was in touch while I was writing my story.

My brother Nino who seized an opportunity to record the TV Channel 4 film on Maxine Sullivan *Love to be in Love* (8.2.95), giving spirit to the title.

Maggie Robinthwaite of Bishopston Lets and Sylvia Jarrett for typing this book.

The staff at Minerva Press for appreciating my writing.

Hannah Wright aged nine for sharing happy times on Brandon Hill and naming my child sculpture JOYIA.

Contents

Chapter One

Early Influences

How old was I? Maybe two years old. So this was 1942. I stood, still and silent, holding on to the wooden bar of my cot, waiting, waiting for something to happen. Listening with all my being and looking out over the side of the cot, I watched over the familiar space of the Cotham Vale front bedroom – there was the wide bed.

The bright daylight joined with my quiet breathing. Beyond the safe warmth of my cot in the far corner, there was no presence in the house. The air was humming. The cot shook so gently.

'Rock-a-bye-baby on the tree top.
When the wind blows the cradle will rock.'

Outside the window was a noisy world – sometimes the sky wound up, exploded and crashed and shook in a zigzag fashion. The banshee wail of the air raid siren merged with the terror of the noise made by our vacuum cleaner, lamenting, lamenting.

The mystery and grief of war swelled together with chilling sound. The year before I was born, Hitler had invaded Poland. Then for us in 1940 began the devastating Blitz of Bristol. During the first raid in November two hundred people were killed and ten thousand houses were damaged. That was the first onslaught, with 167 fires being reported in the city.

My mother told of walking home with Father from my grandmother's house. 'The air raid warning sounded,' she said. 'I began to run after him, pushing you in the pram, desperate to reach the shelter before bombs started dropping. You were bouncing up and down in the pram, your father and me running through the streets towards the shelter, just in time.'

On the December sixth raid, a high explosive bomb struck the platform at Temple Meads station alongside the 7.10 p.m. train to Salisbury. There were heavy casualties when the train derailed. One hundred people were killed during this raid.

After heavy and persistent bombing on 16th March 1941, St Michael's church was set on fire. Three hundred people sheltering in the crypt escaped unharmed, whilst St Barnabas' church crypt had a direct hit and fifteen people died.

An enormous bomb was dropped in the heart of the city on 28th August 1942. Three buses loaded with passengers were set on fire and forty-five people were killed. Nearby, a ninety-three year old woman was found sitting shocked in her kitchen, with part of her shop in ruins.

That was Bristol, the city that I love. The bombing, fires, and destruction of fine buildings and churches left craters, desolation and scars for years long after the war ended. That evoked in me a deep desire to build and restore my city.

After the last raid on 15th May 1944, Winston Churchill, as Chancellor, visited the University. Seeing academic staff with gowns over soiled uniforms worn during the previous night's onslaught, he said, 'I see the spirit of an unconquerable people,' recognising a turning point in the history of the world.

Yes, the war bequeathed that fine spirit, as well as slaughter and ruin: a Phoenix group soul-rising again from the ashes.

Reece Winstone tells of these events, when the air raid warning siren sounded 359 times between June 1940 and April 1941.

Nannie, my grandmother Nina, said 'Switch on the vacuum,' when I cried or screamed. 'No, no likie vacuum cleaner.' The loud voice of *me* was swallowed up into the vacuum. The cleaner lived in the cupboard under the stairs, near to the air raid shelter next door.

'There was a little girl and
she had a little curl
Right in the middle of her forehead.
When she was good
She was very, very good
But when she was bad,
She was horrid!'

Nannie probably first recited this rhyme to me and this teasing verse made me angry: if I was not good, the siren wail would wind up the sky, so the cross feeling must be squashed down, not shrieked out.

'When we lived at Waverley Road,' remembered Mother, 'I put you out in your pram in the garden. Newspaper kept you quiet, so I gave you the *Daily Mirror* to play with. When this neighbour came to the door, she told me "Your baby is chewing newspaper." I was so annoyed because I had to take it away. Then you started screaming.'

Nannie's lodger Miss Dembow often told me later what a bad-tempered small child I had been. 'You were in such a temper, always crying or screaming,' she said accusingly whenever we met. I knew she did not understand my crying, so this story annoyed me.

'You were a Spring baby,' Mother said. 'When you were born in March I almost called you Primrose.' A narrow escape! Yet it pleased me, my being born on the first day of spring, a blossoming time.

Glyn was a musician, playing the trumpet and cornet. He was my Daddy, born in Maesteg, South Wales. Glyn met my mother, Margaret Rose White, when he found lodgings at her parents' home in Bristol. Margaret was attracted to this handsome twenty-four year old musician. They shared the love of music. As she was unhappy living at home, Mother became pregnant, hoping that her parents would agree to early marriage. However, she ran away to Portstewart, Northern Ireland in August 1939 to marry my father. Glyn was playing in a band there at this time.

Margaret was nineteen when I was born at Bristol Maternity Hospital in Southwell Street, Kingsdown, on 21st March 1940. 'The night before you were born,' she confided, 'I had a strong urge to do our washing. There were piles of clothes to be washed. I could not finish the washing because my labour pains started about ten o'clock.'

My parents later went to the hospital. The building was reputedly infested with cockroaches. Mother said that the ward was like a prison, with rows of beds and high windows so that the new mothers could not look outside.

Margaret remembered how when she cried out in pain, the midwife said 'Be quiet or you'll wake Matron.'

'Bugger Matron!' shouted my young mother, spurred on by the energy and effort of childbirth. Fortunately my entry into the world was rapid. I was born at 3.45 a.m., just two hours after Mother arrived at the hospital.

'My pregnancy seemed unreal,' said Mother. 'You were like a doll to me. I had one matinee coat knitted for you!' Nannie hurried off reproachfully to buy napkins and nightgowns. She also chose a white chariot pram for me.

Glyn came to visit us, carrying a bunch of flowers.

'I bought these daffodils for your mother,' he told Margaret. 'She already had some, so I brought them for you!'

A Welsh nurse looked at me in the crib. 'What a large stomach this child has!' she exclaimed. Then, 'Why don't you call her Morveth? It's a lovely Welsh name!'

Glyn and Margaret chose to name me after their favourite black American singer, Maxine Sullivan. For years Maxine's song *A Brown Bird Singing* was played in our house. Later the record was broken during one of our frequent moves. The Brown Bird is an English folksong like a tender lullaby. The poignancy of the message unfolded very slowly through time.

> 'All through the night time
> There's a little brown bird singing,
> Singing in the hush
> Of the darkness and the dew...
> Would that the song of my heart
> Could go a-winging,
> To you.
>
> All through the night time
> My lonely heart is singing
> Sweeter songs of love
> Than the brown bird ever knew.
> Would that the song of my heart
> Could go a-winging
> Could go a-winging, to you.'

Maxine Sullivan was born in Pittsburgh, America in 1911 and died in 1987. Coming from a musical family of ten, she was singing all her life. Maybe earlier years of drudgery, scrubbing floors and working as a waitress added joy to her singing life. She became a great artist and singing star. Maxine became a spiritual mother and soul sister to me, although we never met.

Listening to her songs now I relive the swing era of the 1930s and 1940s which influenced my parents. Maxine was a wonderful, relaxed swinging singer. Some of her lyrics remind me of my father.

> 'Wrap your troubles in dreams
> And dream your troubles away.'

and

> 'Wrapped in the arms
> of sweet romance.'

Her warm lilting voice has a timeless quality, sometimes plaintive with nuances of longing and loss. Lively, vibrant, and loving music and the people to whom she sang, Maxine Sullivan is an inspiration to me. Apparently she began a second career when fifty-eight years old, following marriage and the birth of her daughter Paula.

One of Maxine's famous songs was *Loch Lomond*. Her repertoire was infinitely varied. She sang every song from her heart and soul.

I still love to hear her voice, husky, tender and evocative. Maxine Sullivan reached me through her singing, influencing rapport and friendship with black women.

As I became aware of my body I discovered a raised brown birthmark: it was puzzling to find this fat little cushion of brown skin between two toes on my right foot. Although Mother was not religious, she explained imaginatively to me, 'When God was making you, he did not have enough white skin to finish your foot, he gave you some brown skin.' So the birthmark was a gift, a desirable part of myself.

Here is my Memorial of Baptism card, illuminated with a gold cross outlined in red. Flowers spring from each corner. The card is grubby. A child has scribbled little spirals at each end of the cross.

I was the first-born child. Although my parents were not religious, a christening was expected. They took me for Baptism at St Mary the Virgin church, Tyndall's Park Road in October 1940. As I grew up, I felt that my parents had given me to the Church. My sister and brothers were not baptised.

Mother gave me a second name, Joyce, after her friend Joyce Waters who was my Godmother, so I became Maxine Joyce. The Godfather '…was Bob Hope's cousin!' Very soon the family lost contact with these godparents, I wished that they would come to see me. The words of the Baptism card became a promise to follow. Faithful soldiers and servants I could understand, like in *Onward Christian Soldiers, Marching as to War*. The war was part of my early life, sin and the Devil were puzzling. I did not understand how sin fitted in with being a soldier and a servant. What did sin really mean?

Mother liked reconstructing these early years with me. 'I kept giving your father salad to eat,' she remembered. 'One day he lost his temper and told me "I'm not a bloody rabbit!" So then I learned how to boil an egg.' Gradually she became a good cook.

Margaret was young, very attractive, lively and loved music and dance halls. Every week she went to the cinema where she dreamed, and ate sweets or chocolate. Looking after a baby was too demanding, so she carried on with her own life.

What happened between us when I was small? Mother remembered, 'I was pregnant, with Peter. Something was wrong at home. It seemed to me that having another baby would settle me down and make us into a family. You were so heavy. I was breathless when I carried you up to the cinema gallery to see *Bambi*. That was the first film you ever saw, a sad story as Bambi's mother was killed. When we arrived home, I had to eat a bowl of cornflakes before I'd even taken my coat off.' She had a craving for cornflakes during this pregnancy.

On the bus, an older woman watched her struggling with me in a protesting mood. 'Never mind, dear,' she said to Margaret, 'They soon grow up.'

'I had no idea what she meant,' said Mother, seemingly unaware of a struggle to cope with her toddler.

Mother assured me that she had bought for me a lovely expensive dress embroidered with flowers. A photograph was taken at Brights' store in Queen's Road, Clifton.

Yes, here is the little girl with the curl in the middle of her forehead, looking out bright-eyed for the engaging photographer and fingertips exploring the scratch feeling of wood when touching the table.

When my mother died in 1993 I found this photograph with others in her handbag. Towards the end of her life, Mother carried around that image of her first daughter as she was unable to carry me around during my infancy, touching the roots of her life.

There is a wealth of family photographs, yet only one picture of Margaret snapped with her first three children. Early photographs show us posed on our own, like separate branches of the family tree.

Mother said that I was left for hours in my cot or play-pen. 'You had whooping cough when you were six months old. The noise of your coughing kept me awake, so I put you in another bedroom at night.' She laughed ruefully, recognising that this was drastic. 'Your father was angry if he came home and found you crying,' she continued. 'He went to your cot and picked you up.' She seemed surprised by this, as though she was trying to work out what should happen when looking after a baby. Having described how my father rescued me and gave me attention, she added jealously, 'One day Glyn was holding you. He dropped you and you banged your head on the coffee table.'

Looking at a photograph of Daddy in his early twenties, I see a handsome Welsh man, evocative of a Jewish background. A smartly dressed musician holding a cornet, the first instrument he had played. He faces the world with tentative hope, his expression gentle and sensitive. A fine musician, a dreamer, who evoked strong love and inspiration in the heart of his little daughter.

I was devastated by Daddy's inevitable departure when my parents separated in 1945. Our loving connection continued but our relationship was influenced by separation, loss and longing for reunion. I believe this experience was painful to my father as well as to me. He wrote to my mother saying 'Please let the children write to me. They are more important to me than anything else.'

Separation can act like a dream illuminating essential experiences and aspects of life. Clarity of vision ultimately emerged for me from the experience of distance and separation.

Here is Mummy's American Red Cross Identity Card dated July 1943. Margaret Davies worked for the Red Cross initially as a voluntary helper, and dance hostess, then became a paid stenographer.

I see a lovely, clear-eyed twenty-three year old woman with hair piled high over her forehead. Her expression is serious, a little anxious. I loved and admired her deeply, at a distance. There is a hint of the waif, a certain lostness. Her jaw is angry. My mother was a remarkable woman, strong, innovative and unconventional. These attributes she passed on to me, together with her love of cinema and music, and an interest in travel and other cultures.

After I was five years old my mother's attitude towards me became often angry, critical and rejecting. This followed the pattern of cold resentment she experienced in relation to Nannie from the same age. I am glad that during the last few years of her life we grew closer, enjoying time together. Even though my mother said then 'You are not like me,' she sought my company and showed affection for me. I gained wisdom in relation to my mother – I shall always love her.

Margaret as a young married woman had two children. She felt orphaned, wanted a life of her own, and then found enjoyment in the dance hall of the American Red Cross, meeting young servicemen far from home. This influenced our lives profoundly, leading to the birth of our sister Carolyn in December 1944. Her father is James Andracchio, a drummer of Italian-American descent. Carolyn was raised, like many other wartime babies, as a child of the marriage. As adults we learned of her true identity. Concealing the truth was damaging. Carolyn had a right to know who her Daddy was, in order to know the person she truly is.

Many years later Mother told a sad story of going to meet James in 1944. His friend turned up to tell her that James had been posted overseas – there was no time to say goodbye – James had to leave before his daughter was born.

In 1993 Carolyn finally contacted and met her father and his family in Philadelphia, USA. Mother died in June, just before this meeting.

Carolyn's meeting with James was powerful. 'It was grounding to touch my father. He has the same satin smooth skin. I took his hand and thought, "that's me". My Uncle Joe looks so like me physically that everyone was laughing.' Carolyn realised how different she would have been if James had brought her up as an Italian in Philadelphia. She appreciates that Mother recognised and allowed her stubbornness. 'My father is too like me. We both want to win.' Carolyn prefers that she grew up in England with us, even though she felt something was missing, 'I felt like a half chick.'

James had returned to America, missing Margaret, his first love, and then the baby daughter he had not seen. When he saw a newspaper report that a woman named Carolyn Andracchio had been raped, he contacted her and later married her. My sister met the American Carolyn who made her welcome. Carolyn Andracchio died soon after this visit. Now my sister keeps in touch with James, her brother Vincent, and sisters Roseanne and Carol.

Mother needed someone to understand her: she could not begin to understand me. When I was old enough she began to tell me the experiences which she needed to confide. I was like a wireless, picking up her wavelengths and messages.

Here is one story which Mother shared with amusement and a hint of pride. 'You began to talk at an early age, and spoke very clearly. When you were two, you listened to the names of Russian Generals on the radio and imitated them. We would tell you, "Say Vorishelof, Maxine," and you repeated "Vorishelof". Our family doctor was fascinated. He came to the house one day just to hear you saying those Russian names.'

In the light of later experiences I questioned relatives who confirmed Jewish descent known to my Grandfather James Davies. 'Yes,' said my Auntie Prue, 'Dad knew there was a Jewish branch to our family.' Unfortunately they did not claim this heritage. Yet Jewish ancestors undoubtedly influence my life experience, suggesting a connection with Russia and Poland. Amongst them, a father and mother of musicians.

Chapter Two

The Breach

On 8th April 1942 my brother Peter James was born. 'He looked like a skinned rabbit because he was about two weeks premature,' Mother remembered. His birth was induced early. Mother continued, 'You went to stay with Gran Davies while I was with Peter at the Chesterfield Nursing Home in Clifton. Gran offered to look after you, but you did not know her. You cried so long that Nannie had to fetch you and keep you with her. Then you settled down.'

Jealousy emerged when Peter came home. 'I was holding the baby,' Mother told me. 'You came into the room with your hand behind your back, then you threw the dustpan and brush at him. So I pushed you away. You fell over and began to cry. Then Glyn came in and picked you up.'

Another day I walked into the kitchen where my mother was working. 'She wants a drink of water, she does.' Mummy gave me a cup of water. Carrying the cup out into the garden I poured the water over my startled baby brother, then I tipped up the pram so that Peter swung out suspended in the air by his pram straps. He must have been older then. 'Yet you soon loved him,' said Mother, 'and as you grew older you were happy playing together. That is, until he learned how to bite, and you began to pinch him in return. When I looked at you then – you were two years old

– I said to myself, "Well, she's finished now." I believed that the job of starting you off in life and looking after you was over. When I changed your nappies, Peter had a tiny bottom, and yours was so large in comparison that I thought "She's a big girl now."'

By now it was 1943. Peter and I sat together on the solid wooden sideboard, dangling our legs over the drawers where family stuff was kept. Daddy dressed me in my woollen siren suit, whilst Mummy dressed Peter. Here was the only time I remembered a cosy feeling, being happy that we were all together. The living room was so familiar yet something unusual was happening. I was excited at being dressed to go out after bedtime. I felt safe, being so close to Mummy, Daddy and Peter.

We walked into the basement air raid shelter next door. The cosiness had gone because there was so much space around us, with a stone floor through which I might have fallen if a bomb dropped. A neighbour encouraged me to walk up the steps and look at the sky. Reluctantly I was persuaded to climb the twisting basement steps towards the street.

Planes droned overhead like giant bees. The reverberating sound terrified me. I was fascinated by the bright lights searching and crossing the sky. Where was *Twinkle Twinkle Little Star*?

I stood absorbing this experience, feeling scared in my tummy, and soon ran back down the steps into the shelter.

A vast gap soon opened in my life. Mummy went to work as a stenographer for the American Red Cross, still also involved as a dance hostess meeting servicemen.

Daddy was away playing in a regimental band, somewhere in Belgium. On one occasion, when he returned home on leave, he was annoyed to find Peter and me alone in the house at night.

When I was about three years old and Peter one year, Mummy arranged for us to live with a farmer and his wife, George and Edith Winter of Milton Farm, Nailsea, near Bristol. They had also taken in some schoolboys evacuated from London.

It was Easter time when the little girl was taken with her baby brother to live with Aunt Edie and Uncle George on the farm at Nailsea. Mummy did not tell her why, or for how long she would be away from home, just after her third birthday.

Maxine stood silently in the large unfamiliar kitchen with stone flagged floors and the scrubbed pine table, disbelieving that Mummy was truly leaving her in this strange place with people she had never seen before. Already she had learned that it was wrong to hold out her arms to Mummy when she wished to be loved, so she held her arms back, touching the wooden table. Maxine was a good girl; she did not cry, so that Mummy would love her and return to take her home. All her being called out to cry and scream, 'Mummy, Mummy, don't leave me.' Her arms were rigid, she tensed her legs, seized with shock. The crying, the words, the passion to resist, to protest, went somewhere deep down inside her.

Maxine found a way of not being there, so that she felt no pain when Mummy went away. The door closed.

Most of that time was simply blanked out of memory, although later holidays on the farm offered a familiar background.

The air raid siren was wailing again, even out there in the countryside. I was running up the cobbled yard towards the safety of the white house. This was like a dream, where I kept running and would maybe never arrive. I do not remember arriving but running, as fast as I could, over the cobbled stone to reach shelter, inside the house.

This may have been the day a bomb dropped in a field across Pound Lane. It did not explode, yet this bomb left an image, like a photograph printed at the heart of the world.

Chapter Three

Daisy, Daisy

By December 1944 Peter and I had returned home.

I awoke one morning to the deep long ago atmosphere of Nannie and Papa's house at 30 West Park. Peter was beside me, a small ash blonde boy, sitting up in the double bed near the door.

Nannie came into the room. 'You have a baby sister,' she told us in a pleased to tell you voice. Carolyn Rosemary was born on 18th December – a Christmas Baby.

After this, when we stayed at Nannie's house, she left a biscuit or a few sultanas beside our beds to keep us quiet when we woke early in the morning.

Daisy came some days to help look after us at Cotham Vale. On the radio a song was often played for Daisy:

'Daisy, Daisy,
Give me your answer do.
I'm half crazy
Over the love of you.
It won't be a stylish marriage,
I can't afford a carriage,
But you'll look sweet
Upon the seat
Of a bicycle made for two.'

Our family atmosphere was in the kitchen, mixed with the smell of washing and boiling napkins. Mummy gave me cod liver oil, which was loathsome. I tasted the thick fishy mixture, revolted, and refused to swallow any more. There was orange juice in special bottles from the clinic, far more friendly. The watery orange taste was pleasing. I loved the thick, sweet texture of Malt Virol too, rolling it around on my tongue.

We had ration books. The grown-ups talked about cheese coupons and butter ration. We ate dried eggs and pompotato – dried potatoes from packets. There were clothing coupons and a fascination about how they added up. Were there enough coupons left in the book?

One day I wet my knickers. There were no clean pants so my mother took me to buy new ones at the draper's on the corner of Aberdeen Road. The shop was crammed with skeins of bright wool and other attractive goods. There were counters with hundreds of reels of cotton in trays behind glass. The shop was solid, yet I felt so strange. Mummy and I were out shopping, near to the Co-op with the fascinating wooden boxes which moved about whirring so fast on wires and close to the baker's where Nannie bought good brown bread. I had no knickers on. My bottom and legs were exposed to the air. Something could reach up my legs and touch my nakedness. Someone might see that I was bare, not covered. I felt unsafe.

I woke up during the night. Mummy usually left the light on in the pantry and the light shone through a window into my bedroom. Tonight it was dark. My bed was wet and cold. The darkness and wetness frightened me, so I cried loudly. Daddy padded into the room, wearing his underpants. I noticed his bare hairy legs. Daddy put a blanket over the wet sheet. Settling into the blanket space was comforting. He covered me and went out, leaving the pantry light on. After that, when sometimes I wet the bed, I covered the sheet with the blanket myself, and went back to sleep.

There was a battle of wills with my mother. Mummy smacked me. 'That didn't hurt!' I said defiantly. She smacked me again, harder. 'That didn't hurt!' A third time Mummy slapped my hand, harder still. She won. I cried. I did not oppose her again. Instead, I sulked. That was not allowed either. 'Take that look off your face, or I'll smack you, big as you are! You look just like your father,' Mother told me. She never smacked me again. I knew that I must obey her.

Suddenly I was at Oakfield Road Day Nursery. Sitting at a table with children singing grace, I felt lost and scared.

> 'Thank you for the world so sweet,
> Thank you for the food we eat,
> Thank you for the birds that sing,
> Thank you God for everything.'

A milky, rubbery smell comes back with the memory of clean linoleum-covered floors and rows of pegs in the hall with pictures above them, for hanging coats. I sat still, a mug of milk on the table in front of me. How impossible to drink the cold, tasteless stuff. Someone took it away.

It was rest time. We all lay down on small folding canvas beds, like in camping. A grey woollen blanket covered me; it felt rough like Daddy's army blanket. I lay on the bed, wide awake in bright daylight. Other children slept. At home we never had a rest in the afternoon.

Daisy boiled Carolyn's Viyella nightgowns for a long time. Mother had embroidered flowers on them. The nighties went yellow.

Daisy went away.

Chapter Four

White Blossom

Light and darkness, day and night followed each other in a happier atmosphere at our Cotham Vale home. In the bright living room there was a radiogram for Mummy and Daddy to play their music. The little brown bird was singing: this is my song because my name is Maxine.

There were french doors opening out on to the garden. A beautiful tree grew just outside in a corner against the grey stone garden wall. The fragrance of fresh white syringa blossoms magnetised and drew me to bury my face in the abundant petalled flowers.

Tuesday 8th May 1945 was VE Day, though I did not understand this at five years of age. On this day of sunshine there was jubilation in Bristol, with church bells ringing to celebrate the end of the war.

Whole streets of little houses and shops had been destroyed, like Bridge Street and Dolphin Street: the heritage of generations lost to the people of Bristol. Historic buildings had been blasted and demolished: the 15th century St Peter's Hospital, once home to a wealthy merchant, was one of the fine buildings reduced to a heap of rubble.

Now the war was over. The beautiful Church of St Mary Redcliffe near the port was packed with joyful people. Many Bristolians must have paused to read again the words inscribed in the porch:

'From this Church the merchants of Bristol sailed their fleets and explorers set out to discover the New World.'

Now I know that my great grandma, then Emily Rose, her sisters Clara Sophia and Matilda, and brother Horace were baptised at St Mary Redcliffe in the 1880s. The Roses lived in Pile Street, alongside St Mary Redcliffe church. My great, great, great grandmother, Sophia Harvey, was a midwife, born at Chew Magna, and had still been helping mothers give birth to their babies when in her seventies, in the Redcliffe area.

Today bunting and flags were strung across the streets, and pianos were wheeled outside. The greatest of many bonfires, twenty feet high, was built near Blackboy Hill on Durdham Down, and fireworks were set off. A Nazi swastika flag was flown at half-mast on the flagpole of the Bristol Royal Infirmary. All over Bristol men and women danced on their air raid shelters.

Although unaware of many events I felt clearly and distinctly the change of atmosphere around me. I absorbed peace and stillness, and relaxed. The war was over: no more mournful sirens winding up the droning bee planes in the sky. In Cotham Vale we all enjoyed a street party, with a large bonfire. I wandered amongst the neighbours milling everywhere, eating crisps which salted my tongue. The grown-ups were in a happy mood and kept laughing at each other.

As darkness fell every light was switched on around the City. This was an amazing sight, especially from the hills above Bristol. The black-out of wartime was ended and everyone rejoiced in the return of light.

On a warm day following the party I played happily in the garden, wearing only white pants and enjoying free movement of my bare legs and feet. It was blissful playing with water, filling bowls and stirring tins with Mummy's spoons, and kneeling on the grass, absorbed in mixing earth puddings, with streams of water everywhere. Mummy was there, somewhere in the house. The damp growing smell of rich earth reached me as I stirred and patted the puddings.

Time was now as it had never been before – peaceful. The war had ended.

Chapter Five

The Monkey Puzzle Tree

Nannie and Papa, my Grandparents Nina and Robert White, lived at 30 West Park. Their house was close to our home in Cotham Vale. Most days we lived between the two houses, walking to and fro.

The Monkey Puzzle tree grew in Nannie's garden. This tree was a mystery. Standing still, I gazed up towards strange hairy branches, spreading outwards and reaching towards the sky. The Monkey Puzzle was different to other trees. I picked out the blobs of gum collected along the tree trunk, squashing them softly and stickily between my fingers. The tree filled me with wonder – it belonged to the beginning of everything, its roots and branches connected to the secrets of the world. I know now that Monkey Puzzle trees were popular in Victorian times. The tree is also known as the Chile Pine.

The White family moved to West Park in 1935 – my mother Margaret, her sister Eileen and small brother James. Today any passer-by can still see a marble lodged in the grating on the front steps. This was done by Uncle Jimmy when he was a little boy. This house keyed me in to family history. My mother told stories there of her own childhood. Nannie's influence was powerful. I was sensitive and open to the strong atmosphere linked to the past: no other house offered the same messages as West Park.

Nannie told us rhymes and sang songs as she sat with baby Carolyn half-wrapped in the dark green waistcoat which matched her skirt. Carolyn had a lovely mass of dark curls and large eyes. She gazed solemnly at the world but loved to dance, jumping up and down and clicking her tongue when music was played.

> 'Shall the moo cows have her?
> Shall the moo cows have her?
> Shall the moo cows have our Carolyn?
> No, No, No!'

This lullaby with a veiled threat, accompanied by continuous patting of the baby, moved through a range of potentially marauding animals before it ended.

> 'Shall the horses have her?
> Shall the horses have her?
> Shall the horses have our Carolyn?
> No, No, No!'

The living room next to the kitchen had a table with a long green plush cover, Victorian style. Nannie's sugar basin said 'There's mair where this cam frae' in flowing letters. When Nannie poured the tea, sometimes she recited the magical poem of a fairy in her tea cup,

> 'I took her out
> And dried her
> And asked her if she'd stay,
> Oh No! she said I mustn't
> And then she flew away.'

Papa cleaned my shoes for me in the living room. He was not often there, yet was friendly. At the centre of the room was Nannie, sorting everything out, sewing much needed garments and telling stories. She was a wonderful cook who liked preparing family meals. Roast potatoes and beef with Yorkshire pudding, carrots, greens and thick brown gravy was a traditional favourite, followed by apple pie and custard. We had orange and blue dishes patterned with fruit, for special days such as when we ate delicious Christmas pudding containing threepenny bits, and later sixpences, carefully hidden to surprise us.

Nannie especially liked egg and tomato sandwiches. She hard-boiled the eggs, soaked the tomatoes in hot water to remove the skins easily, then mashed the eggs and tomatoes together for brown bread sandwiches. These accompanied us on any outings to the seaside at Weston or Bournemouth.

One day a parcel arrived from friends in Malta. Inside we found dark, sweet Bourbon biscuits which we had never tasted before because of wartime conditions. I enjoyed this special treat, eating all around the edges of my biscuits with tiny rabbit-like bites and saving the chocolate until last.

Jelly I liked to eat in the same way, even though it tasted the same in the middle, savouring the wobbly slippery sensation of jelly in my mouth.

> 'Jelly on a plate
> Jelly on a plate
> Wibble wobble
> Wibble wobble
> Jelly on a plate.'

I inherited a thick china porridge bowl from either Mummy or Auntie Eileen, which had a picture of Rock-a-bye-baby on the tree top,

> 'When the wind blows

The cradle will rock
When the bough breaks
The cradle will fall
Down will come baby,
Cradle and all,'

chanted Nannie. Peter's bowl had a picture of a boy pilot coming in to land, and was ordinary. My bowl had messages and secrets behind the baby in the cradle. I liked my porridge bowl. Sometimes I tilted it so that rivers of milk ran away from the baby, then I could look at her tucked into her cradle in the tree top.

Nannie rarely spoke of her family. Once she took me to Blackpool to visit her sister Lily. Before we travelled on the train I was given a good fish meal. 'An empty tummy leads to travel sickness,' Nannie explained.

In Blackpool I lay in bed in the morning listening to donkey bells as the animals were led to the sea-shore.

Down in the kitchen a dead hen was suspended from a hook. I was horrified, 'Who did that?' I asked indignantly. The grown-ups thought that it was funny that the hen was dead, and laughed. The chicken was for our lunch.

Before we returned to Bristol Nannie took me to a show where I was entranced by a pool covered with beautiful floating lilies.

At home again Nannie told Peter a warning tale of his namesake, a Peter who teased people by crying 'Wolf', then, when the wolves came and chased him, nobody believed his cry or came to help him. She taught us a poem remembered from her own childhood, which she recited in a special voice.

'Molly had a shilling
She bought a little mop
When she started mopping

> She found she couldn't stop.
> She mopped the dog
> She mopped the cat
> She even mopped
> Her father's hat.
> When her mother came home
> I don't know what she said
> But the mop went in the cupboard
> And Molly went to bed.'

Molly the mopper puzzled me; such a busy person who cleaned the house yet ended up in disgrace.

Papa remained a shadowy figure in the background, until one day I met him on the upstairs landing. 'Be very quiet,' he said. 'You can come in here with me.' I was surprised, but followed him obediently into the lavatory. Papa stood just inside the door and showed me his penis. This thing looked ugly to me, very large and hairy. However, Papa was proud of this part of himself. He was pleased, standing there with his penis in his hand. 'Touch it, go on,' he urged me, smiling. I felt frightened, fascinated and repelled at the same time. Instinctively I knew that touching was forbidden. Gingerly I reached out and tentatively touched his penis. 'Don't tell Nannie, or anyone,' he said. Quickly now he ushered me out and downstairs.

I did not tell. The incident lodged in my mind and body, a bewildering secret.

Papa became ill soon afterwards, lying in a twin bed in the back bedroom. Papa was a seaman, like his great grandfather James Dyer. During the war he was in the Navy and his submarine had been torpedoed. Papa had '…a weak chest.' He was sixty-one when he died just after my fifth birthday.

Papa was once Bertie, the little boy in the old family photograph who had been upset because he had argued with his sister Agnes about a boat, and great Grandfather James had taken his boat away. Bertie was the young boy sent to an orphanage during his father's long illness. James White, we discovered many years later, died in Bristol Lunatic Asylum with encephalitis. He too lost his father when young, at the age of eight years. Kind, sad James whose family life cast so many shadows down through the years, after he died at the age of forty, alone in the asylum.

Soon after Papa died I stole sixpence from the stocking for the Blind in the hall of Nannie's house. Walking around the corner to Abbotsford Road I bought a raspberry ice lolly. I liked the watery sweetness of ice lollies, sucking until the lolly numbed my tongue. Nannie found out because her lodger, Mr Hunter, had put the sixpence in the stocking, and had told her that the money was missing. 'There's a police car waiting outside to take you away,' Nannie told me when I returned. I was frightened, but the policeman never came to the door to ask if I was there. I expected him to knock at any time.

Another day, some girls were playing in Cotham Vale. Penny knocked at her mother's door, crossed her legs, then hopped up and down. 'Mummy, I want to do a motion.' Knock, knock, no answer. 'Mummy I want to do a motion!' The words she used fascinated me as we called this going to business. The girls were distracted by the event.

In a corner of a doll's pram was the bag of bright yellow sherbet. I picked up the bag and walked away, dipping my finger in the sherbet, sucking it, and enjoying the sharp taste. Later that morning as I walked towards Nannie's house, there was still some sherbet left in the bag. In West Park I saw three girls coming towards me. I felt guilty and dropped the bag by a wall.

'We've been to tell your Nan on you,' said one of the girls accusingly. I said nothing but knew the police would be outside the house again soon.

Chapter Six

His Master's Voice

Nannie carried a bowl of steaming water into the living room and put it on the table. 'Lean over the bowl,' she said, placing a towel over my head. I had another sty. The attention Nannie gave me probably helped to cure the series of sore red spots which swelled up on my eyelid. Inhaling the steam, covered by the towel, there was a brief aura of security.

Once, Daddy had leave from the army when a sty bothered me. His return home, his presence, was reassuring. Daddy was cheerful and playful with me. He brought home a grey blanket to make my bed cosy.

Near the radiogram was a pile of records which Daddy and Mummy played. Some had a label saying 'His Master's Voice,' and a picture of a dog listening to an old gramophone. This dog was real to me, as though he belonged to us. The Brown Bird song was friendly, different to other songs, and all through the night time, a little bird sang. On the other side of this record was *Dark Eyes*, a beautiful Russian song.

Suddenly, Daddy was gone. We did not say goodbye. I did not see the door close. The five year old girl did not understand that her mother and father had separated. Her back felt strange, as though people were moving about and hiding behind her, a creepy feeling like something crawling over her. When she turned round to look, nobody was there.

A man came with a brush and covered the old walls with white paint.

Many years later my father played a song which told me why there was no goodbye.

> 'My heart would break
> If you should wake
> And see me go.'

Glyn the musician had a remarkable career, travelling the world, leading his own band, and later working at sea on the liners of the Shaw Saville Group.

Glyn, my beloved father, was born in Maesteg, in the vale of Glamorgan, South Wales, the first-born of six children. Glyndwyr, his given name, means clear water. My grandfather, James Davies, was also a fine musician who played cornet and trumpet, and became a band leader. He was a man of reconciliation and of peace. Grandmother Eleanor had a fine contralto voice, and was a dressmaker. How I wish that I had heard Eleanor sing in the choir, 'like a lark in summer'.

When the family moved to New Tredegar, Daddy began to learn cornet, playing with the Salvation Army Band, as Grand-dad James had done. He progressed to the Penallta Band, and Grand-dad arranged for the conductor, Mr Stevens, to give private tuition to Glyn.

On Daddy's eleventh birthday he received the gift of a silver-plated cornet. Recently he told me, 'I remember vividly, running home from school to occupy the hallowed front room, the parlour, to practise. I was encouraged to enter traditional solo contests, and at age thirteen won my first medal playing a favourite called *Zelda*, written by Percy Code, an Australian. I was accepted as a member of the fine

Yorkshire Bentley Colliery Band. A year later I joined the Munn and Felton Band, Kettering, now called the G.U.S. Band and in 1934 they were world champions.

'My parents had moved to Salisbury, so I decided to play with the Salisbury City Band and enjoy some home cooking. However, with a switch in musical direction I began to play with a dance band led by Ron Percy. When we played for a function at Salisbury Town Hall, the visiting band came from Bristol. I was offered engagement with the Freddy Williamson Band. We were kept busy with functions such as police and hospital balls and weddings, and regular broadcasts from the BBC studios in Whiteladies Road, Bristol.

'A summer season with Reg Owen's Band at Portstewart in 1939 was cut short with the outbreak of war. So I returned to Bristol and played at the Hippodrome under the direction of Syd Phasey.

'In 1942 I was called up for the armed forces and went to Beverley, Yorkshire for primary training. Then I was sent to Devizes, to join the Wiltshire Regimental Band, playing principal trumpet. After service in Belgium, I was demobbed in 1947.

'Next I formed my own band, spending the summer in Bournemouth. After returning to London I was offered a contract to lead a five-piece band on the Shaw Saville liner *Dominion Monarch*, calling at the Canary Islands, Capetown, Fremantle, Melbourne, Sydney and Wellington, New Zealand. We broadcast from studios in Wellington. I spent several years on Cunard and P and O liners, seeing much of the world.

'My next contract was playing at the Waldorf Restaurant, Capetown, doing three band shows daily. We also played for Greek and Jewish weddings.

'I went on to Los Angeles, then Philadelphia. As you know, in Philadelphia, an accident ended my playing, when I fell, knocked a front tooth out and damaged my lip.'

I remember now, with pride, the wonderful flowing quality of my father's music. The tone and range of his trumpet playing, a wide repertoire of music from classical to dance music.

Above all, I remember the early rainbow music of Ivor Novello – magnetic, evocative words and sound of my earliest years – *Fold your wings of love around me*, and *Waltz of my heart*, from the Dancing Years.

> 'I can give you the starlight
> Shades of shimmering blue…'

and

> 'Rose of England –
> Proud and Bright from rolling year to year.'

Also *Fly home little heart* from King's Rhapsody.

> 'Fly home little heart
> Your wings are brave and strong
> Fly home where you belong…'

Some of this music I heard on records played by Mummy and Daddy. Daddy's musical world flowed into our home.

> 'We'll gather lilacs in the spring again
> Until our hearts have learned to sing again –
> When you come home once more.'

Daddy had gone, leaving a waltz in my heart which nothing could change; leaving an outward flowing pattern which I rediscover when I dance today.

His postcards, letters and visits became a lifeline for me. When Daddy came home I felt alive – in his absence my feelings were buried below the surface of everyday life.

The Master's Voice dog was my pet now, linking with a time when Daddy lived at home in between wartime separations. Now I know the story of this dog.

Nipper the dog was a Victorian character who became famous across the world. He was a mongrel bull terrier born in Bristol in 1884, the time of my great grandparents, James and Emily White, who lived in Bedminster. Nipper's master was Mark Barrand, a theatrical artist, and the two became inseparable. Nipper sometimes joined his master on the stage of the Prince's Theatre, Park Row, to take a bow.

Mark Barrand died in 1887 leaving a widow and five children and his brother Francis gave a home to Nipper. The dog became fascinated by the family phonograph and he sat listening to the horn loudspeaker, with his ears cocked. Nipper and Francis moved to Kingston on Thames where the dog died in 1895 and was buried beneath a mulberry tree in the garden. Three years later Francis painted a picture of Nipper, in memory of a dearly loved pet.

This painting was sold to a gramophone company for one hundred pounds. In 1908 Nipper replaced the company's original logo, becoming a famous pet. The record company was named after the picture, *His Master's Voice* – and Nipper, still listening for His Master's Voice.

Chapter Seven
Tonsil Pie

I began to have colds frequently, so I wiped my nose until it was sore and red, or sniffed. My mother talked to our doctor and decided that I should have my tonsils out. In 1945 children often had their tonsils and adenoids removed as this surgery was intended to prevent frequent sore throats or colds.

One day Mummy took me to the Chesterfield Nursing Home in Clifton where Peter and Carolyn had been born. In Matron's office everyone was having a friendly chat. 'There is a nice bed waiting for you,' Matron told me. 'Would you like to come and see?' As there was such a happy atmosphere, I was curious to see where this bed was, so Mummy and Matron took me along the corridor to the ward. The bed turned out to be very ordinary, so why were the grown-ups so pleased with it?

A sinking feeling came into my tummy. It was disappointing to find that I was expected to get undressed now, and stay in the hospital without Mummy. It was daytime – not the right time to go to bed. My intention had been just to see what the bed was like, since Matron found it so promising, then go home again.

I did not speak or try to protest. The sinking feeling deepened as I began to take off my shoes and socks. During the night I wet the bed and woke up crying for my mother. A woman in the next bed called out to me. Nurse came and curtains were drawn around the new bed. She did not say that she was cross about changing the sheets – she did not talk much. 'I want my doll,' I said. It was impossible to say that I missed my mother. Nurse gave me the doll and I cuddled her because she might be frightened.

Next morning I was crying and struggling as a long rubber tube was pushed up my bottom. Yes, as a child, I protested more about that enema than about anything else. It was unbelievable that such an invasive, horrible experience could happen to me. The tube felt tight, as though there was no room for it, yet Nurse ignored my resistance and continued pushing the hard tube higher up inside me. Soon after this ordeal ended I felt very sleepy. Someone wheeled me, half awake, on a trolley down the long passage.

I woke up with a sore throat. When I swallowed my throat hurt, yet I could not stop swallowing. Later, Nurse gave me ice-cream and jelly which was soothingly cold and sweet. Now in a larger room with other children I watched the doctors making their rounds. How frightened I was, looking at the strange, sharp-looking silver instruments they used. I did not want the doctor to look at my throat with a silver hook. Maybe I would choke, or be smothered, so that I could not breathe.

At visiting time, Mummy and a friend came to see me. I was pleased to see her and felt safer, so I tried sitting on the pot. I was constipated. The rubber tube had stopped anything coming out of me. I felt tight inside my bottom. 'Where are my tonsils?' I asked. 'Would you like to take them home in a jar?' Mummy asked me. 'Yes, I would rather keep them with me, not leave them behind in the hospital.' However, Mummy found out that the cook had made my tonsils into a pie!

Before I left hospital a doctor looked at my throat. I was so relieved that he did not bring a knife or a funny instrument. He used the handle of a teaspoon, so I did not mind showing him the place where my tonsils had been. He must have been a kind man who understood the fears of children and noticed my nervousness.

So now it was time to go home. I could not take my tonsils with me. Someone must have eaten them.

Chapter Eight

Amberley Days

Pamela, standing next to me, cried loudly, 'I want my mummy.' It was our first day at Amberley House School. We were in the busy basement cloakroom, surrounded by chattering children, navy coats on pegs, and shoe bags.

This little girl crying for her mummy astonished me. What could her mummy do if she came back? Why was Pamela crying like this? I was so often with other people that starting school was just another change in life.

The smell of coats, wellingtons and rubbery indoor shoes merged with a new experience of children singing hymns, and milk crates at playtime.

Amberley House stands on the corner of St John's Road and Apsley Road. Miss Scammell, the Head Teacher, named her school after the lovely village of Amberley near Stroud.

In 1945 we lived at 40 St John's Road. I ran to and fro on my own, returning home for lunch. Early school memories merge with Sunday School at St John's Church nearby. There was the light in the dark when I went to bed. At St John's Church, there was light in the dark too – a notice outside told me so – this was all part of the hymn which we sang at Sunday School.

'Jesus bids us shine
With a pure clear light
Like a little candle
Burning in the night.
In this world is darkness;
So let us shine
You in your small corner,
And I in mine.'

Many years later I discovered that the lives of my Somerset ancestors, the Whites, revolved around St John's Church in Bedminster when they first moved to Mill Lane from Wiveliscombe around 1840.

At home there was no religious influence, although Mother was respectful of religion. Officially we were Church of England, but my family were not church attenders. Mother sent us to Sunday School so that she could have peaceful times on Sundays.

For my sixth birthday I was given a lovely grey doll's pram, and managed to cajole an afternoon off school in order to wheel it up and down St John's Road. I also received a Noah's Ark with attractively carved wooden animals. I played on the carpet in the comfortable half-circle of the settee, setting out the lions, tigers and two white doves.

At school the story of Noah and the Flood impressed me deeply, above all, the return of the dove with an olive leaf. The dove hovered above the flood waters, showing Noah and the animals that they were approaching land, and all would be well.

In our classroom there were groups of small tables and chairs. Above us was a mantelpiece with a clock on it; so school seemed like Miss Scammell's house. The atmosphere was safe, calm and well-ordered. We had two teachers. I remember mainly Miss McKenzie who, when she was cross, spoke sharply like a sword.

One day I was being a cat, miaowing like a cat. 'Go outside,' I was told firmly. There was a large grandfather clock in the hall, ticking in a regular, soothing way. Later on, Peter, in his turn banished for naughtiness, tried in vain to hide behind the clock so that I would not see him and tell Mummy. I took my older sister role seriously. When I moved on to Form One, I went to the kindergarten to ask Miss McKenzie how Peter was getting on. She was amused and told me, 'Peter has settled happily in the classroom.'

Letters and words came naturally to me. I soon knew the early simple reading books. Amongst their pages I discovered bright pictures and clear black words. There were dull tales where Ned was urged to see Baby, and Rover to fetch the ball; Jane and John always helped Mother and Father. Little Red Hen was my favourite – I met her living on the farm. Little Red Hen scurried about, seeking grains of wheat, taking them to be baked into a loaf – baking bread to eat, like the good brown bread which Nannie gave us.

I loved the small copy-books and happily wrote on soft pink pages. We learned to write over letters and sentences, then to form our own letters. Writing in those books satisfied me. Gradually the pink books led on to green ones, each one more advanced. The green books had a colder atmosphere, lacking the supportive structure of the pink ones, where tracing the shape of letters and sentences, and completion of the task was assured. Eventually we found ourselves transcribing alone such phrases as 'Rome was not built in one day,' below the example set out in a flowing hand.

Numbers bewildered me sometimes. One day I kept writing number '5' as the letter 'S'. Over and over again my '5s' emerged as 'Ss'. 'Go up to the big girls' class,' Miss

McKenzie said. As a punishment I was sent amongst the big girls to learn that I must write '5' not 'S'; that I must grow up as quickly as possible, and that I was not a baby now who could continue to write 'S'. The older girls were amused by the diversion of a kindergarten child appearing amongst them. I sat at a large desk feeling shy and confused, aware that girls around me were smiling and staring. I was in disgrace and frightened by the teacher's reaction to my dilemma. Yet it was interesting to be in a new class. The girl nearest to me was Daphne. She was wearing snow-white socks, and her hair was arranged carefully in sausage curls. I sat and wrote 'S' that looked like '5' and '5' that looked like 'S', feeling increasingly confused. Most of all I wanted to write 'S' because I liked the shape; it was curly like smoke and drew me like a magnet.

Sometimes we played singing games in the basement playroom where assembly was held. The room was large and the light was dim there. Crates of empty milk bottles and crushed straws reminded me of playtime. I always refused milk, feeling repelled at the sight of a child eagerly drinking the cold liquid which to me was undrinkable. I was afraid of being forced to drink milk, but nobody there made me drink it.

The game which I liked best was *Here We Go Round the Mulberry Bush*. We all walked around in our circle, boys and girls holding hands, singing and pushing on,

> 'This is the way we wash our clothes,
> On a cold and frosty morning.'

This was a familiar and reassuring activity, accompanied by busy gestures. The circling continued for a long time, then the game changed.

'I sent a letter to my Love
And on the way I dropped it.
One of you has picked it up
And put it in your pocket.'

This game worried me because the letter was lost and we would have to find out who had taken it, otherwise the message would not arrive. The words were poignant and stirred something within me. 'It isn't you, it isn't you, it is you!' All was well once the letter had been found; after the suspense of wondering and waiting.

Afterwards, we played *The Farmer's in his Den*. This was real because Peter and I lived with the farmer, Uncle George. That day I had to be the bone, which was hateful. I stood in the middle and everyone patted me. 'We all pat the bone, we all pat the bone, ee I ee I, we all pat the bone.'

One day we were prepared for Princess Margaret's visit to Bristol. 'We are going to welcome her,' our teachers said. Later we all walked to the corner of Apsley Road, then lined up by the wall on Whiteladies Road, the main road leading to the city centre. After a long wait and much fidgeting, an open, sleek black car drove by. Princess Margaret, a lovely lady, sat on the back seat, smiling and waving. We cheered, waving our tiny Union Jack flags as Princess Margaret Rose passed. I knew she was Margaret Rose, just like my mother, because Nannie had told me so. I loved to see photographs of the two little princesses, Elizabeth and Margaret, in magazines, partly because I was fascinated by history, partly by their beauty and part-associating them with the childhood of my own mother and her sister, my auntie Eileen. I was magnetised to their carefully donned pretty dresses, buttoned shoes and neat socks. The Royal nannie in the background watched over them. Two other little girls from a past which I could never reach were evoked by stories which Mummy told me, needing my understanding.

After waiting for so long, Princess Margaret's visit was quickly over and we returned to the school.

As I grew older I was more aware of our teachers. The Head, Miss Scammell, was a mountain of a woman and seemed enormous to me. She wore glasses and plain, full, dark-coloured dresses. One of her frocks was navy with white spots. Her manner was quiet, yet firm: she reasoned with disobedient pupils. Miss Scammell remained a background figure, contributing a sense of security to me and I liked her gentle voice.

We children were amazed by her size; we invented rhymes about her.

> 'Fat Miss Scammell
> Rides on a camel,'

called out Angus, a carefully tended little boy in buttoned shoes, as he scampered down to break. It puzzled me as to how Miss Scammell managed to have a bath. There was a bathroom near her ground floor office, containing a small hip bath. However did she get into it, and once in, how did she emerge again?

Regardless of the teasing, the children liked her – she understood children. Miss Scammell succeeded in building a good school which offered sound education. Lack of a playground imposed a limitation on physical activity and all-round development, so the children were taken by coach to local playing fields for games.

Miss Dennis, her deputy, was opposite in character: she was thin, tense, wiry, very active, with grey hair screwed back into a bun. Miss Dennis rattled her teeth as she spoke, clicking to stress a point, rather like marbles being knocked together. She was keen on spelling, and emphasised morals.

Mrs Homeshaw was the kindest of all the teachers; I felt safe in her classes. She was a happy woman who did not pounce on children in her care. Mrs Homeshaw listened, cared about us and, through kindness, kept order by expecting us to behave well. I liked school work with Mrs Homeshaw.

Miss Porteous had been a missionary, as she liked to tell us. She had bulging eyes and wore glasses. Miss Porteous was impatient and bad-tempered. Unfortunately she taught me arithmetic, and when I could not do my sums one day she scolded me. This did not improve my arithmetic so she hit me on the arm – I was frightened by this violence.

That night I told Mummy, 'Miss Porteous hit me because I could not do my sums.' 'Did she indeed!' said Mummy indignantly, 'Well, I'll see about that!' Whether or not she complained to Miss Scammell, I don't know, but Miss Porteous did not stay long. I was glad that my mother had stood up for me.

She told me a story of her friend Lilian. 'When Lilian was a little girl she had a teacher called Miss Tapp who used to hit the children with a ruler. One day her father went to the school. "Is your name Miss Tapp?" he enquired. "Yes," she responded eagerly. "Well, if you touch my kid again I'll bloody well tap you," he told her.' The message was clear. No teacher was going to hit Margaret's children. She did not hit us, and had smacked me only once for being defiant at four years of age.

Morning assembly was part of changing seasons and festivals. The singing influenced me deeply. *All Things Bright and Beautiful* still evokes the atmosphere of children singing at Amberley House. I expressed whole-heartedly through song feelings which were inexpressible in conversations at home, or with others. As we sang I imagined the tiny flowers opening, and birds flying amongst the trees. The rich man in his castle overshadowed the poor man waiting at the gate. The poor man wandered hungrily by with a sack across his shoulders – he was probably cold too.

Why was the 'Green Hill without a City Wall'? This hymn aroused a serious sorrowing feeling; it was very mournful. Another hymn which evoked very strong imagery was Samuel's song,

> 'Hush'd was the evening hymn,
> The temple courts were dark,
> The lamp was burning dim
> Before the sacred ark.'

The temple was so real; I was there, within its walls; I saw the temple, in lamplight; the flickering shadows; the hushed atmosphere; the ancient stone pillars.

> 'And what from Eli's sense was sealed
> The Lord to Hannah's son revealed…
> …Oh! Give me Samuel's heart.'

At Christmas we gave a concert for parents. I sang one verse alone, timidly. I was about seven years old. I could see trees in the Green Wood and the fleet-footed deer, yet I was standing in the kindergarten room surrounded by people. There were butterflies in my tummy as I sang,

> 'The Holly bears a blossom
> As white as the Lily flower,
> And Mary bore sweet Jesus Christ
> To be our own Saviour.'

What a relief when everyone joined in the chorus, and the deer were running again.

To follow, there was the Skye Boat Song which was my favourite. I stood swaying a little, as if to help move me forward like a boat.

'Speed Bonny Boat
Like a Bird on the Wing
Onward the Sailor's Cry.
Carry the lad who was born to be King
Over the sea to Skye.'

The sea was like a vast blue lake. The rocking of the boat, as I swayed, felt like a lullaby. But then there were rough waves, and the wind 'howled' as I tried to carry the Prince towards freedom.

By now I was eight years old, and we had moved to 9 Clyde Park in Redland. Sometimes, money was in short supply so we lunched at home. Peter and I would return to school by walking up Whiteladies Road, and across on the other side an orderly crocodile of Amberley House Children returned to school after lunch at The Copper Kettle Cafe. Sometimes we joined these children and enjoyed the meals, especially steamed pudding with custard.

On one occasion our freedom from routine led to exuberance. Joyfully we chanted as loudly as possible, above the noise of the passing traffic, across the wide space of the main road,

'The copper kettle's boiling,
The copper kettle's boiling,
Take it off and make the tea,
The copper kettle's boiling.'

This was followed by a summons to Miss Scammell's office: such unseemly behaviour in public could not go without reprimand, yet Miss Scammell did not speak harshly. Maybe she was amused by the rhyme which I, in an unusual outburst of energy, had invented.

Chapter Nine
Zoo Rescue

Mummy planned to make strawberry jam. 'You and Peter can go to the Zoo' she said, taking a large saucepan out of the cupboard. She gave me the money for the entrance tickets.

As we walked along Beaufort Road towards the zoo, I pretended to be mummy, walking on tiptoe, wearing imaginary high heels, pushing a fantasy pram. Peter walked beside me, trailing his hand along the wall. I imitated the sound which Carolyn's pram wheels made on the pavement – 'Damden dooge, Damden dooge' as we went along.

We loved the zoo. Alfred the gorilla was our first favourite. He became a celebrity in Bristol, having arrived in September 1930. Alfred loved children, performing obligingly for his audience, peeling a banana and jumping around his cage. Daddy took us once to see Alfred, which made the gorilla special, so that day we went as usual to watch Alfred playing.

Alfred died in 1948 and was greatly missed by many Bristolians, so the Authorities stuffed him. He can still be seen in the City Museum where we later continued to visit him.

We then wandered on to the Monkey Temple. Peter and I were fascinated by the antics of the monkeys, chasing, scratching and grooming each other, meticulously searching for fleas. The highlight was definitely when some of the monkeys displayed brightly coloured bottoms to their cheerful young audience. I puzzled over the absence of fur around these vital areas. Surely their bottoms were cold in winter? The outrageous rudeness of their casual behaviour, defying the usual taboos about bottoms, was impressive. I stood gazing thoughtfully at the monkeys as they scampered around in the pit of the Temple.

Leaving the monkeys we walked around the duck pond. This pond at that time appeared to be the size of a great lake. I was watching the ducks swimming around, and Peter was picking up leaves around the edge of the pond. Suddenly there was a splash and a cry. Turning quickly I saw my little brother immersed in this lake. He kept going under, and rising, spluttering to the surface. There was a look of horrified surprise on his face. I stood stock still, frightened, wondering how to rescue Peter. An elderly man nearby swiftly rolled up his trouser legs, waded in and mercifully pulled Peter back to shore with his walking stick. What a relief. We were not going to lose him after all. Another man wearing smart uniform appeared swiftly on the scene. Very soon Peter was installed in the St John's Ambulance hut, wrapped in a blanket and given a hot drink and I was despatched to alert my mother. It seemed a long way home, although not far in reality. Down Guthrie Road, across Pembroke Road, then breathlessly through Beaufort Road, I rushed as fast as possible to break the news to Mummy.

She was in the kitchen, making jam. A large pan of red liquid bubbled on the stove. 'Mummy,' I gasped, 'the ambulance man has got Peter.' Mummy abandoned the jam, destined not to gel.

We returned to the zoo. Peter was sitting on a bunk in the little hut, in his element, with a blanket wrapped around him. He was the centre of attention for the St John's man, who probably was bored by long periods with no action. He now had a purpose and was talking to Peter as he drank his cocoa. After the alarm caused by his accident it was surprising to find Peter in a cheerful state, being cosseted by the St John's man and the rescuer with wet trouser legs.

We spread runny strawberry sauce on our bread. It tasted good.

Chapter Ten

Mr Collins

Mr Collins appeared when we were living in St John's Road. He arrived on a motor cycle whenever Peter was naughty: Mr Collins was real to us but we never saw him.

Mummy and her friend Lilian gave us spaghetti for lunch one day. 'Here are some worms from the garden,' said Mummy joking with me. 'I don't like worms,' I said, glad of an alibi for not tasting new food. The spaghetti remained in a pinkish heap on my plate.

Mummy was laughing, telling Lilian about the new divan bed with spring interior mattress which she had bought me when we moved. 'She calls it her spring material diving bed!'

At St John's Sunday School we sang:

'Jesus bids us shine
With a pure, clear light,
Like a little candle
Burning in the night.'

The vicar told us that we could do nothing without the help of God. This was suspicious. How could God possibly do everything for me? There was a step between the living room where we ate, and the kitchen. After careful reflection I decided to risk testing the truth. Tentatively I said to myself, 'I can go down that step without the help of God.'

There, I had done it, even though I wondered whether God might strike me dead or something like a flash of lightning might happen. Just as I thought – there were some things I could do without the help of God.

Peter had taken his pedal car out of the garden, which he was forbidden to do. 'Mr Collins will be here any minute to deal with you,' Mummy told him. I was mesmerised, waiting for Mr Collins to appear. After parking his motor bike and side-car, ready to take Peter away, Mr Collins would come through that garden gate wearing his black leather jacket, helmet and goggles. Perhaps he would take me too, for saying I could go down the step without the help of God. Peter ran into the house to hide. I waited in suspense for some time, feeling scared. Mr Collins was so real that I imagined his standing by the garden gate.

Mr Collins did not arrive. He remained on call until we went on holiday to Bournemouth, then he stopped coming to our house.

Chapter Eleven

The Broughty Ferry

Sitting in the cinema I was absorbed, marvelling at the story of Pinocchio, the little wooden puppet. He had had so many adventures before he became a real boy. Seeing Pinocchio braving the depths of the ocean and singing his special song moved me deeply.

> 'When you wish upon a Star
> Makes no difference who you are
> Anything your heart desires
> Will come to you.
> If your heart is in your Dream
> No request is too extreme.
> When you wish upon a Star
> As dreamers do.
> Like a bolt from out the Blue
> Fate steps in
> And sees you through.
> When you wish upon a Star
> Your dreams come true.'

Towards the end of 1946 we moved to Bournemouth, living for short periods in rented houses at Branksome Manor, Canford Cliffs and Somerset House. We also stayed for a while at the Broughty Ferry Hotel, as Mummy knew the owner.

Looking back, I recognise a family link with the past. Great Grandmother Emily Rose's ancestors came from Scotland, and Broughty Ferry is near Dundee. The Ferry once ran from the harbour across the Firth of Tay to what is now Tayport. There is a castle dating from 1490 sited on an old Pictish fort. The English held the castle for three turbulent years until a Franco-Scottish fleet recaptured it. Always, it seemed that my spirit clung instinctively to roots of the past, even though I had no clear understanding of connections at the time.

Now the security of the Broughty Ferry carried me across another gulf in my life. We had no settled home, there were frequent changes, and I felt lost, often in a state of dumb misery. Even though Mummy was around we did not talk to each other unless Mummy wanted me to do something or was enraged by something I had done, so I was unaware of her problems.

It was December 1946. We were driving from Bournemouth back to Bristol to spend Christmas with Nannie at West Park. That winter was severe, and the roads were covered with snow and ice, slippery and treacherous. Suddenly the black Ford car skidded out of control, landing on its roof with a sickening thud. I found myself upside down, and the silence was broken by my cries of fear. Carolyn, my two year old sister, was also crying loudly. Fortunately none of us was hurt and we were soon helped out of the car. There were several car accidents on the same road near Bath that day. Somehow we travelled on to Bristol.

Having survived the crash without injury, we arrived in confusion, and as we climbed the front steps of Nannie's house Carolyn fell down and split her lip open. The little girl's hurt and bleeding mouth needed Nannie's experienced attention.

There is blankness after this. I remember a holiday at the Broughty Ferry before we moved from Cotham Vale. Mummy found two young friends to accompany us and their task was to look after us on holiday. One of the young women was Pauline who had just celebrated her twenty-first birthday. Twenty-one years seemed so old to me; it also seemed an age which I could never reach myself, so I expected to die before I was twenty.

We had some happy times on the wonderful sandy beach at Bournemouth, playing with sand and water, paddling in rock pools, catching tiny crabs and popping seaweed. Yet Mummy was not with us there. The young friends returned home after a few days, following an outing to the park instead of the beach to where they had been instructed to take us.

There was another holiday when I was about eight years old. Often I went to the beach in charge of Peter and Carolyn. One day I took a set of spare clothes for Carolyn, aged four, then encouraged her to wade into the sea so that she would be wet. 'Go a little deeper,' I urged her. Now she was wet up to her knees. Soon the waves splashed her blouse. Now I could change her and make her dry and comfortable. This gave me a sense of security; I was mummy.

On the beach I met an older girl named Molly. She was clever at building a sand-castle with firm walls and splendid turrets, then digging a moat all around it. The glory of the castle she crowned with a small paper Union Jack flag. I admired Molly, and was fascinated by her creative digging and building. After this I looked forward to seeing Molly on the beach and was disappointed when she was not there.

One day a great wave drenched me as I waded into the sea and Molly's mother emerged from the family beach hut. She wrapped a large towel around me, drying my face gently. This was so comforting, and I felt safe and looked after, with the towel wrapped around me, talking to Molly's mother.

Then came a holiday when Mummy had a new boyfriend called Wallis Burridge. His mother and sister Christine accompanied us to Broughty Ferry. Christine and I were the same age and shared a bed. One morning I woke up and Christine was sitting up in bed beside me. She laughed, 'I can see your bum,' she said. I felt embarrassed by this unexpected exposure, and pulled down my nightie quickly. Mummy was somewhere else with Wallis: we never went to her room.

That day, Christine's mother took her riding with Peter. The idea of riding a horse scared me, so I stayed on my own, feeling lost and lonely. I walked up and down the promenade for a long time, hoping to find Molly and her mother.

After this holiday Mummy arranged to go to Malta with Wallis. Her friend, Lilian, looked after Carolyn: Peter and I went to a boarding-school in Bournemouth.

Chapter Twelve

Grains of Wheat

We arrived out of nowhere. I cannot recall the house we left on the day on which Peter and I travelled to Nether Hall – possibly it was the Broughty Ferry Hotel.

Crowded into the old black Ford with our belongings, we arrived in great haste. The shops would soon be closing, so there was a rush and scramble to buy dancing shoes for me. There were no soft leather ballet shoes like the pink ones previously chosen for me to go to Miss Maddocks' classes in Bristol.

Once, there had been a lovely Studio room with mirrors. The Dancing School was in West Park, near Nannie's house. Miss Maddocks had taught me how to curtsy, 'Curtsy One, and Curtsy Two, with a smile.' In between, my face remained serious with the effort of remembering how to curtsy, Mother had told me later.

Now, I had hard, pointed red party shoes; the wrong shoes worried me more than going to boarding-school. Nether Hail was a square solid building on a main road in Bournemouth, busy with traffic. A cold greyness like fog surrounded me from the time we entered the door.

What had happened with Mummy? She barely said goodbye, just went quickly out of the door. I could not feel any belonging to her now – just this empty, foggy grey space all around me. Peter was here with me; we both stood there silently, waiting for something to happen.

Behind us the lavatory door knob rattled. A little girl had locked herself in, and could not open the door. She shouted, 'Let me out, let me out, open the door.' A tall woman bustled around, and soon the gardener, wearing dark overalls, appeared. 'Fetch a ladder,' the teacher said, 'Jean has locked herself in the WC.' What was that? Jean banged on the door. Would she have to stay inside? The door suddenly opened, and out came Jean and the gardener who had climbed through the window. The teacher ushered us into the play room with Jean.

Soon it was tea time. Sitting at a big wooden table I saw large plates of bread and butter, rock cakes and huge jugs of milk. I never drank milk, yet a mug stood in front of me, full of milk. Children all around me at the tables ate hungrily. They chattered, seizing eagerly on the mugs of milk, gulping as they drank. I felt frightened, dreading that the teacher would force me to drink the milk. That was impossible.

I began to cry. The teacher was cross, 'Go to the play room for being so silly. Stand in the corner until you stop crying.' I was in disgrace but relieved to get away to the quiet play room. The clock ticked on the wall above me. The children's voices were far away. It felt like being on an island, with space all around me instead of water.

The children returned and played around me. Soon a little girl told me, 'If you are naughty and you fight with your brother, they knock your heads together.'

Another day in the play room I was surprised when a parcel was handed to me. Auntie Eileen had sent drawing books and coloured pencils. Some love came to me, far beyond the brown wrappings in my hand; a lifeline with home.

Our class teacher, Mrs Davidson, was kind to me, and praised my reading. There was a large wall chart in the classroom. Mrs Davidson tested me, pointing with a thick ruler to the black words. I soon read the chart and most of the reading books. Reading satisfied me; my teacher liked me. Several times I won the weekly class prize for good work, usually some sweets.

The story of the Little Red Hen and the grains of wheat was offered to me. Hens were my friends from early days spent on the farm at Nailsea. I love hens.

'Who will help me to plant the grains of wheat?' asks the Little Red Hen. 'Not I,' say the animals. 'Very well, I shall do it myself, says the Little Red Hen. When the wheat is reaped, the same process happens again. Little Red Hen takes the grains of wheat to the baker and soon she has a delicious loaf of bread.

The lesson ended, and we trooped off to the hall for a dancing class. The music was lively, yet I felt so strange that I could not respond. Moving about with the other children, I pointed my toes, making obedient little jumps and turns, yes, puppet-like I pranced around as if from mechanical strings. The greyness was back; the space around me was vast, empty and cheerless. The final parade around the room, ending with a curtsy to the teacher, was a relief, then a short passage of freedom, running down a path outside.

The Matron, Miss Crusoe, was strict and cross. The children were her *trouble*. There were rules, and stars were given if your bed was made neatly. Miss Crusoe kept lists behind the bathroom cupboard door, but I won no stars from Miss Crusoe. When she was off duty Mrs Davidson gave me a star. 'Maxine Davies has a star!' exclaimed Miss Crusoe incredulously when she returned. 'Well, as you are a big sister, you must wash your socks and your brother's too!' As I had never washed socks before, this was worrying.

It was bedtime. The children queued up in a long line, wearing dressing-gowns, waiting for a quick wash. When it was bath night, I was bathed with a boy called Brian. I did not know him, and found this strange and embarrassing. One day a girl felt sick. I was scared. 'Will she get to the toilet in time?' It seemed ages before she was hurried away, without sick on the floor.

Another day, Jean had a tummy pain. Jean had locked herself in the lavatory the day on which we had arrived and had to be rescued. Now she groaned and cried, twisting about on the wooden bench. Miss Crusoe gave her some fizzy Andrews in a glass. I was frightened – maybe the pain would never go away – yet Jean soon recovered.

A horror was still to come. Every morning we lined up in front of Miss Crusoe and she pushed Vick up our noses on the handle of a teaspoon. 'This will stop you having colds,' she told us. My tonsils had been taken out to stop colds! How it burned, the Vick, searing upwards in my head, alarming me most because I could not stop Miss Crusoe doing this to me. I cried loudly in a way which I had never done at home. Miss Crusoe always closed the bathroom window in case some passer-by should think that children at Nether Hall were ill-treated.

It was so hard to sleep at night – summer time and still broad daylight at bedtime. We lay in our iron framed beds in the dormitory and there was no talking. In my head was blankness, just time and light stretching endlessly ahead, and I tried to sleep.

One night Mrs Davidson came into the dormitory with a friend who was visiting the school. Standing beside my bed she smiled and said proudly, 'This is Maxine.' I was glad, and puzzled. Mrs Davidson came to see me in bed, she wanted her friend to know me; Mrs Davidson was pleased with me.

Soon afterwards Miss Crusoe called me from the play room. 'A visitor is coming to see you. Go to the laundry hamper and fetch clean blouses for yourself and Peter.' I went up to the bathroom and fished about amongst the contents of the hamper. How could I find our blouses among so many? Defeated, I returned to Miss Crusoe. Disapprovingly she followed me back to identify the blouses.

I cannot remember the visitor arriving. We returned home soon after this. My mother brought me a pretty flowered cotton dress from Malta. It was a larger size than my other dresses, ready for an older child.

Chapter Thirteen
Angel at the Bridge

Peter and I returned for some school holidays to Milton Farm where we had lived during the war. Carolyn joined us once or twice but said firmly that she did not like being there.

There is so much to tell of that time – rich experience of country life – yet a missing dimension. I resist returning in memory, to vast fields where I walked alone, telling myself stories. I wonder how to write about the void opening when I remember Nailsea, then dream of a little girl.

This child was not fair like me; she had dark hair and brown eyes. She was seven or eight years old, standing alone in a vast open space. Who was she? I remember the photograph of Auntie Nancy, Daddy's sister. I recall a picture postcard of a little Irish girl washing clothes in the river. She looked cold and lonely, her mother had died and she wanted to run away.

Yet no, this was a little Jewish girl, her name was Rebecca, but her papa called her Riva. This child haunted me most. 'My mama died,' she told me. She travelled to many cities with her papa – Warsaw, Berlin, Amsterdam, then Paris. 'Always travelling, moving on,' said Riva. 'We came to England on the ship, to London, my papa and I. We left our home and our country; I never could go back. I longed to return and find Mama, but I knew she was dead.

Her name was Mira, my papa is Daniel. I was born near the Polish border.'

'Why are you so sad?' I asked her. 'I have no home,' Riva responded. 'No mama to light the Shabbat Candles, say Kaddish for Mama.'

When I return to my childhood experience of separation from home, mother and father, I see clearly now the reflection of other childhoods before my own – childhoods in Eastern Europe – who were they? What happened to them? An older more distant experience shadows my own: voices speak to me from the past. Riva, my mother Margaret, the little Irish girl Eileen, Flora of Scotland long ago, Emily Rose my great grandmother, Marguerite of Normandy; I am the seed of all these children come home to me as witness and mother.

Above the large brass railed bed where I slept were two coloured prints of angels. My own dear Angel beckoned the way across a bridge. She wore pink flowing robes, and as I turned to see her before I slept, I felt safe.

One night there was a thunderstorm. Lightning flashed outside the window and thunder crashed overhead. Aunt Edie came into the bedroom, 'Don't worry,' she said. 'It's only the babies falling out of bed in Heaven.' I puzzled over her meaning, comforted by the Angel who was so near me that I was aware of her presence emanating from the image above my head.

On Sundays we walked along Pound Lane to the Methodist Sunday School about a mile away. The church was a building of solid grey rock like stone. The hymn which I most liked singing was

> 'Build on the rock
> And never on the sand.'

Molly built wonderful sand-castles on the sand at Bournemouth. Of course, the sea always washed them away, and the soft grey west country stone remained standing.

The white farmhouse was solid and comfortable. Downstairs there were stone flagged floors with rush matting and colourful rag rugs. The light from the oil lamps gave a softened quality to our surroundings in the darkness.

When I visited St Fagan's Folk Museum at Cardiff in 1993 there was a cottage bedroom furnished like my bedroom at Milton Farm. A religious text, framed on the wall, the flowered jug and basin on a wash stand and the nearby brass bedstead with a fringed cotton counterpane all recreated an atmosphere which caught my heart in love and pain. There was a security in Nailsea life which was absent at home. This farm was home to me when I was young, and Aunt Edie gave physical care which was also missing in my own home. I realised then how the way of life on the farm had keyed me in to the lives of ancestors long ago – to a rural England and village life before the great exodus to the cities, and to English, Welsh and Irish ancestors who were farmers. In 1996 I discovered that my great grandfather, George Stack, had farmed in Kerry. There we were with an 'Uncle' George in Somerset, and nobody ever talked about great grandfather George in Liverpool. Did mother know they were farmers?

We were well fed. For breakfast we ate raw Quaker Oats with milk and sugar. The jolly man on the packet wearing black clothes left a presence with me too. At lunch time we often had wedges of meat pie with cabbage and swede, sometimes mashed potato and bacon sandwiches. At tea time we might have slices of bread with syrup from a green Tate and Lyle tin, with a lion on the front. Underneath were the words,

> 'Out of the strong
> Came forth sweetness.'

Blackberry and apple pie was appealing because we helped to pick the blackberries, learning how to avoid scratchy brambles and nettles which stung our bare legs. The local children called them 'stingers', beating them back with a stout stick. As we plucked the juicy berries, we ate plenty as we moved along the hedge, and returned with stained fingers which gave us away.

Aunt Edie showed me how to top and tail the gooseberries and blackcurrants grown in the garden. Uncle George said that babies were found under gooseberry bushes. I knew this was just a story – I grew in Mummy's tummy.

At harvest time there were special meals. I carried large cans of tea and bacon sandwiches out to the farm workers reaping in the fields. Sometimes we were allowed to ride back to the farm on the hay wagon which was pulled by horses.

One day I stood in the field where the bomb had dropped, watching a rabbit frantically running as the wheat in the middle was stripped away. Round and round it ran in circles. I pitied the poor little creature with no way to escape. A gun shot rang out in the harvest meadow. One of the men lifted a limp body with furry paws outstretched. A killing. Rabbit pie for supper.

Aunt Edie usually treated us well, although not with affection. Sometimes she suddenly lost her temper and this explosive quality made me approach her warily. One day my loose tooth came out. I wrapped it in tissue and put it under my pillow. At home the Tooth Fairy always left sixpence for a tooth; Aunt Edie was cross at this expectation. She picked up the pearly tooth and contemptuously threw it out of the window into the farmyard. I stood looking outside after she had gone. Where was my tooth now?

During the war other evacuees, from London, stayed with the Winters. They did not return after the war as we did. Aunt Edie was busy and liked us to play outside all day. She was more patient with us than with a little boy named Keith who stayed there. He wet his bed, and in later years developed St Vitus Dance, being unable to sit still or refrain from movement.

Uncle George was busy around the farm and left his wife to look after us children. He was cheerful, good-tempered and full of jokes. I felt uncertain about his teasing. If I came near the cow shed door while he was milking, he squirted milk at me from the nearest teat. I felt exposed and was over-sensitive to ridicule. Uncle George did not call me Maxine; he called me Topsy or Poppy Poo Pah, like one of his cows. I must have seemed a strange, quiet child to him. Occasionally he took us to market in his lorry, and we were fascinated by the smells, crowded stalls and animals.

The Winters had a daughter named Eileen, a young woman then. She was friendly, and at a later time looked after Carolyn and me in her own home.

Every morning Aunt Edie carried hot water upstairs to pour into the bowl on the wash stand. I washed myself slowly, pleased with the flower pattern on the jug and bowl.

Underneath the bed there was a china pot to use during the night. In the daytime we went to the outside lavatory, at the side of the front garden. Sometimes I saw spiders in there, and as they moved so rapidly I remained watchful. There were squares of newspaper threaded on to string, to use as toilet paper.

Nearby was a beautiful lilac tree. The scent of the purple flowers reached me and I liked to bury my face in the mass of petals.

When I became constipated, storing everything up inside me like a hamster, and afraid to let go, Aunt Edie was surprisingly kind to me, just as Mummy had been on two occasions at home when I had expected to be told off. Surely it was naughty not to Go, to be unable to Go, yet they coaxed and encouraged me. Aunt Edie even offered me a pot to try and 'Do Business' indoors. So often I was frightened; now I unexpectedly received attention and understanding.

We were firmly washed, or soaped in a tin bath in front of the stove. Our clothes were thoroughly washed and hung out to dry on the line across the farmyard. Sheets were boiled in the copper standing in an outhouse. I liked the fresh smell of boiling linen as Aunt Edie stirred the copper, then I watched the clean sheets flapping on the line near the cow shed.

When our sandals became too small, Aunt Edie cut out the toe area. She lined them with newspaper so that we needed no socks. 'Your mother never sews on buttons,' she grumbled. Aunt Edie mended our clothes and kept everything in order. I felt that it was my fault that Mummy never sewed on lost buttons: I was mute, as though unable to talk.

Sometimes we received a parcel from home, usually containing chocolate bars. I sucked a Crunchie bar slowly, oblivious to the fact that it made my tongue sore, and was intended to be crunched!

Occasional visits from Mummy were important. One day Peter and I set out to our favourite place, Moore End Spout. As we reached the top of the lane I glanced back and saw Mummy and Uncle Jimmy, distant figures approaching the farm. Even though we turned back and met them, I was haunted later by the memory of almost missing this contact. Mummy came on the bus to see us, with Jimmy. There we were, all together in Pound Lane, walking towards the farmhouse.

Peter and I often played by the stream at Moore End Spout. A flat stone bridge spanned the clear stream which ran on through the meadows. In the distance was the spire of Tickenham Church. Cows grazed in the fields around us, a friendly presence, and when they mooed I enjoyed imitating the sound, calling back to them.

Below the old bridge was a source of rushing water which poured continuously into the stream. The sound of water splashing and murmuring was calming, creating a peaceful atmosphere. We paddled in the water, squirming our toes in the muddy bed of the stream, then fished for tadpoles. All the tiny black tiddlers, teeming with life and darting around when we fished them out, died amongst a trail of weed in the jam jar.

Back at the farm I sat in the dairy, churning milk to make butter, turning the handle until my wrist ached. Peter carried his teddy bear up to the loft where the apples were stored. While I churned butter, seeing the golden fat emerge from the frothing milk, he trimmed Teddy's fur. I was dismayed to see the cloth-covered bear with fur removed. Peter was surprised to find that the fur did not grow again.

My favourite creatures were the hens who became real companions to me. Aunt Edie showed me how to collect their eggs; a triumphant clucking alerted me to possible nesting places. I gathered eggs, brushing off some of the straw and coopie dirt, collecting them carefully in a basket. The comfortable hens scratched and sauntered busily around the farmyard. Sometimes they made nests hollowed out in the earth, or buried into the straw of the cow barn, shedding tiny feathers which I collected too.

I gladly followed the hens around, watching as a brown speckled head was tilted to one side, listening profoundly, then a speculative cawing sound following, as though ruminating on the secrets of the universe. The variation in size and colour of the eggs fascinated me. I preferred the brown eggs dotted with speckles.

There were ducks who waddled about a nearby field, producing larger eggs which we ate as a treat. Chicks and ducklings were raised in coops, a little hut with a run surrounded by wire netting. I loved holding a downy, cheeping creature gently in my hands. I sat absorbed in watching the little fluffy birds, admiring their yellow beauty.

I encouraged a calf to drink from a bucket, by dipping my fingers into the milk. The calf's tongue felt rough, rasping against my hand. Uncle George drove the cows out to the field, calling them by name – Clover, Topsy, Buttercup, Maisie. Peter and I walked around with sticks, lifting the hard skin covering the cow pats they left behind, which usually buzzed with flies.

Often I walked around the fields alone, telling myself stories woven around large families. The most dramatic was *The Highwayman*. In this vivid tale, a woman, married to a highwayman, lived with her five children in a caravan. The offspring slept in folding beds covered with patchwork quilts. Every night their mother placed an oil lamp in the window to guide her errant husband, wondering 'Will he come home?' Inside the caravan the children all waited and listened for the sound of galloping hooves.

I saw the butcher's boy in his white overall cycling past the hedge. 'How can I get into the field?' he asked me. Obligingly, I gave him directions and continued walking. Suddenly the butcher's boy arrived beside me, guiding me into the shelter of the thick hedgerow between two fields. 'Let me look inside your knickers and I'll give you threepence,' he said. I knew that this was dangerous now. Paralysed with fright I began to cry, as the boy kneeled down and reached out to pull aside my knickers. 'I'll go and fetch my little dog,' he said. 'Wait here.' I waited for him to return, unable to run away. Gradually realising that I did not have to stay rooted to the ground, I ran as fast as I could back to the farm. My heart beat so hard that I could not catch up with myself. The butcher's boy did not return. He could easily have been identified in the village. Feeling that it must have been my fault I did not tell anyone about the incident.

We had tea in the parlour with some visitors. 'She tells herself stories,' said Aunt Edie. 'Have you seen her wandering around the fields, with her fingers going?' Eileen laughed good humouredly. They all smiled and I felt very silly and strange.

In the front room of the farmhouse there was a tenant staying with her disabled son Donald. He was tall and heavily built, yet wore a large bib. I was nervous of Donald because he dribbled and made strange noises. He remained a stranger, as I did not understand his way of talking.

The two friendly farm dogs were Bonzo, a brown and white collie, and Patsy, a black spaniel. Keith always seemed to be in trouble. He teased the dogs who were gentle creatures. I told Aunt Edie, so he was in trouble again, but I would not allow him to mistreat the animals.

Once, when Peter and I were playing at Moore End Spout some village children appeared. One boy lingered and urged me, 'Show me your dick, then I'll show you mine.' This was very different to the butcher boy experience. The others were now at a distance. So obligingly I pulled down my knickers and displayed my bottom to him. He crouched down on the bridge, observing my genitals with quiet interest. However, he then refused to show his penis in exchange. I felt cheated in the pact we had made. I ran on to catch up with the other children. They began teasing Patricia, the only other girl in the group. It was tempting to become an insider and make someone else feel left out, so I joined in. Pat began to cry and they all ran off up the lane. Then I felt ashamed, and also afraid that her older brothers might come looking for revenge, so I put my arm around her shoulders and tried to console her as we walked back slowly to Pound Lane. Pat stopped crying and I felt cheerful too.

When it rained I read books in the small living room at the back of the farmhouse. Eileen produced a book called *The Wide, Wide World*. She and Aunt Edie were talking and Eileen said 'Carolyn looks like Bette Davis because she has such large eyes.' I sat on the window seat looking out at the vast grey sky, reflecting on the Wide, Wide World.

A book which deeply absorbed me was Alison Uttley's *A Traveller in Time*. The child Penelope stayed on a farm, too. She '…passed through the door moving to and fro in time,' travelling back to the days of Mary Queen of Scots. 'In my dreams past and present were coexistent, and I lived in the past with a knowledge of the future,' said Alison Uttley. I, too, became a traveller in time, sometimes belonging to the past, unearthing shards of patterned china and blue Nailsea glass in the fields like an archaeologist stripping down layers of human existence. I sometimes turned towards the future, reading the clear visionary stories of Alison Uttley.

There was a sudden end to our link with the farm. We did not return for holidays after I was about nine years old. I visited Aunt Edie once when I was fifteen years old. Carolyn and I lived with Eileen for three months before we moved to London in 1952, and kept in touch with her occasionally until the 1970s.

Now I appreciate the way the Winters shared their home and way of life with us. This yielded a deep love for the country, the rhythms of nature, the life of animals and changing seasons. I grew closer to the process of life itself, the patterns of nature, watching the stream and all around me, than to the people who looked after us.

Close to the farmyard was an orchard full of trees yielding sweet red Somerset apples and juicy plums. Cowslips grew abundantly in the field nearby.

In 1996 before I moved house, my Bristol garden recreated a wild profusion of daisies, buttercups, violets and white moondaisies. Below the willow tree which I planted, a cluster of cowslips reappeared, all reminding me of the beautiful wild meadows and grassy banks of my childhood.

Chapter Fourteen

Strawberry Nets

Judy Moon of long ago, in Somerset: as a seven year old the very moon meaning of her name magnetised and fascinated me, stirring my imagination. There were white moondaisies growing in the lane and in the fields; the moon was bright in the dark night sky; was there a man in the moon?

Judy was a tall fair-haired schoolgirl, maybe ten years old, with an air of confidence. She was aloof, a girl of few words who could easily be whomsoever I wished to imagine. She too had a younger brother. They lived with their parents in a square, white and solid house at the corner of the lane. The Moons had a large garden where Mr Moon grew vegetables and strawberries.

Memories of the lane link with Judy, who became a focus for my vague yearnings and intimations. Occasionally I met her walking with other village children, or with her brother. I wished to be friends with Judy but I was shy and did not know how to talk to her. Judy Moon belonged to the village and lived with her mother and father. I was an evacuee, a stranger from the city, now tolerated as a visitor for school holidays. Judy Moon was a real little village girl who lived with her family.

Judy Moon was swinging on her white gate, the cuckoo was calling, and I stood in the lane, alone. I listened to the cuckoo voice which echoed through the vast clear sky,

'Cuckoo, Cuckoo!' I wondered about the elusive bird which laid eggs in other birds' nests: I puzzled over nestlings which grew fatter and fatter until they pushed out the birds' own offspring and took over the whole nest.

As I lacked friends for my walks along the lane and across the fields, I often invented stories for myself, and characters from stories which I had read became my companions. I also created stories about imaginary families. Fantasy and reality were easily linked.

'Cuckoo! Cherry Tree! Catch a bird. Give it to me.' Nannie said that a bird had flown away with my dummy when I was two years old. 'You never asked for it again!' she told me. The birds took my cherry tree.

Rag and Bone was in the same story book as *Cuckoo Cherry Tree*. Down the lane trudged Rag and Bone, her black rags fluttering like tattered flags, skeleton hands clutching her skirts. 'Rag and Bone! Alone, Alone, Heart of Stone, Alone!' She hated people, and never received a kind word. Rag and Bone was lonely, sad and unhappy. Befriended by Little Girl she thawed and mellowed. Rag and Bone taught Little Girl to grasp a rainbow, catch the wind and carry rain in a sieve. Rag and Bone said one day 'Goodbye Little Girl, some day you will know your heart's desire, and you will find it.'

I wandered the lane between the farmhouse and the Moon house. Along the quiet lane the hedges were scattered with pink dogroses and ragged robin. There were clumps of orange berries. 'They are poison. Don't ever pick them,' Aunt Edie instructed me.

Sometimes I played with Peter. We liked fishing for tadpoles at Moore End Spout, and paddling in the squishy mud. Peter and I found a small snake in the hedge. Was that poisonous? Did it bite? The snake was quick and mysterious. Silently it wriggled and glided away and disappeared.

One day I was invited into the Moons' garden to pick strawberries. The berries were covered with nets. Mr Moon said that the nets were to protect the strawberries, and that sometimes a bird would become entangled in the net. We stood in the garden. I imagined a bird trying to reach the juicy red strawberries and being caught, trapped. If no Moon person came along, the bird would die.

Mr Moon lifted the net so that Judy and I could pick strawberries. We ate our strawberries, smiled at each other and began to talk. The strawberries tasted sweet.

Chapter Fifteen
Roundabout Redland

In 1947 we moved to 15 Elgin Park. All I can remember of this house is my lying in bed with chicken-pox, itching my way to recovery, and trying not to scratch.

We have lived in three Redland houses. My mother had no regular income, often struggling to pay school fees. She raised money to keep us, mainly through buying and selling property, showing enterprise and ingenuity. Sometimes money arrived from my father. On his visits home, various clothes were bought for us – summer sandals, blazers and school raincoats.

Mother found two brothers, Frank and Harold, who were painters. She bought a house which needed renovation, at a competitive price. Along came Frank and Harold to paper and paint our new home, then mother sold the house to make an income, while buying the next one.

Frank and Harold were kind and good-natured. They talked to us, and never said that we were in the way as they worked. Harold reminded me of my favourite gorilla, Alfred, and I pondered over the reason for the resemblance.

One day Mummy took me to visit the Nawawys, Egyptian friends living near Clifton Down Station. I waited alone in a room at the back of the house. Mrs Nawawy was giving birth to her first child in the next room. Out in the yard her husband was catching a hen to cook for a celebratory meal. Mrs Nawawy's cries and groans of pain merged with the loud squawking of the chicken which was pursued and killed by Mr Nawawy. I was frightened by the mysterious pain of childbirth combined with a killing outside. When Mummy returned I remained mute, unable to say how upset I felt. Poor chicken, poor chicken, why did he kill you?

From Elgin Park we moved on during 1948 to Clarendon Road, close to Redland Green with its lovely chapel. Standing at the window, I watched the lamplighter come round every evening to turn on the gas lamps in our road. There was a lamp outside our house. He arrived on his bicycle, with clips on his trousers allowing him to mount and dismount easily. As the lamp man reached up with his stick a glowing light emerged in the dusk. On he went then, to the next lamp.

Inside our house there was still some gas lighting, requiring replacement of the mantles when they were broken. On the bedroom windows were fitted black cloth blinds, to comply with the blackout during the war when no light must be seen from outside. There were also strips of tape across the glass to prevent fragments flying around if the windows shattered.

I was reading a book in the sitting room when Mummy came in. 'Maxine, Emily is crying for you in the dining room because you're not looking after her.' I felt guilty and immediately went to reassure my baby. My favourite doll, Emily, was sitting on the settee: she must have been alive, and feeling neglected. I did not play much with my dolls, yet I was fond of them. I picked up Emily, hugged her and sat down with her on my lap. Talking gently, I said that I did love her, but that I wanted to read my Enid Blyton book. 'I'm sorry I left you on your own. Did you feel lonely?' I asked, cuddling Emily. I did not realise that Emily could feel until Mummy said that she was unhappy. Poor Emily – how could I leave her all alone to cry like that?

It was Christmas Eve and Father Christmas would come if we were good and went to sleep. We had pillowcases for our presents. There were always lovely gifts – Mummy even gave us presents from the cats – as she enjoyed choosing toys for us.

I lay in bed feeling excited, far too awake to sleep. Peter and Carolyn were asleep; I knew that it was very late. The more I tried to sleep the harder it seemed, yet what would Father Christmas do if he found me awake?

Suddenly I heard heavy footsteps on the stairs. My heart began to thud. 'He's coming and I'm not asleep,' I realised. I heard creaking and knocking noises on the landing as Father Christmas shuffled about, heaving the pillowcases around. The door was opening. I screwed my eyes shut, hoping that he would think I was asleep, and buried my face in the pillow.

He was there, in the room. He was Father Christmas but also a stranger like Mr Collins. I did not know him, and his presence frightened me. He was moving about. I felt the bed dip as he swung the heavy pillowcase down at the end. There was a rustling as he sorted out his other pillowcases – then he was gone. Feeling relieved, I drifted off to sleep. I knew that looking at Father Christmas would be like trying to look at God. He did not look at me either, because he did not realise that I was awake.

Early on Christmas morning before Mummy was awake, we all opened our presents. Tearing off the bright patterned paper very quickly we discovered one present after another. Soon there was a mountain of paper around our beds.

I chose a jigsaw from my pile of presents. In the sitting room I tipped the contents of the box out on to a tray, then started to fit the pieces together all around the edge of the picture. This was a garden with vivid green grass, filled with flowers.

I began searching for beautiful gardens as I walked around the city. I loved Bristol and absorbed harmony and security from the soft-coloured stone buildings around me: I was a child of my city. One day in Tyndall Avenue I found a special garden belonging to the university. It was quiet and peaceful and I walked around the gravel paths looking at hundreds of little plants and flowers with labels beside them. I knew that this garden was different; it was a place to learn about some of the plants growing in other parts of the world.

Chapter Sixteen

Hauntings

During the West Park time and into the 1950s when she lived at 19 Cotham Road, Nannie went to Spiritualist meetings. 'I saw daffodils floating in the air around the circle of people,' she told me one day. Nannie was pleased; I was scared. How could flowers move around a room with nobody holding them?

Nannie rarely spoke of her family in Liverpool. During the 1980s I questioned my mother on her own memories, then looked into our family history.

Nannie's mother, Margaret Stockdale, was a baker's daughter from a wealthy Yorkshire family which owned a chain of bakeries. Apparently they disowned her when she married George Stack, an Irish music-hall artist who also worked as a dock labourer. He was born on a farm in Tralee, County Kerry. The couple had eight children who all went on the stage. Margaret often reared them alone whilst her husband, known as Tom, was away on theatrical tours. Nannie had been a dancer before her marriage. My great grandmother, Margaret, died the year before I was born, and Tom Stack died in 1943, aged seventy-one, 'of severe burns accidentally caused by his house taking fire.'

Nannie told me one story of Tom Stack. 'I was very young,' she said, 'and my father carried me in his arms. I looked over his shoulder and saw a ghostly pale woman.'

This story frightened me too. How could a ghost be there? A woman who came from nowhere. Who was she?

Later, Nannie told me a story about a woman who was lying in bed one night. 'She stretched out her hand, and an ice cold hand reached out in the darkness and grasped her,' said Nannie with relish. I was nine years old and stayed the night at Cotham Road. My Aunt Eileen and I shared the front bedroom, sleeping in twin beds. Auntie Eileen was also sensitive, and nervous of psychic phenomena which later unbalanced her when under stress. Although Eileen was in bed and I could hear her breathing, I lay terrified in the darkness. For hours it seemed that I lay rigid with fear, careful to keep my hands under the blankets – an icy cold hand might touch my hair, or it could be searching for my hand in the dark room. If I was asleep the hand might reach out and touch me. Nothing happened, and at last I slept.

Nannie viewed a house in Elgin Park but decided not to buy it because of a strong unpleasant atmosphere in the kitchen. I heard Mummy telling Lilian, 'Later on, she heard that the previous owner killed himself by putting his head in the gas oven.' So it seemed that Nannie was right when she sensed the supernatural in various ways. There was no way to talk to grown-ups and share my fears.

Secrecy surrounded ordinary everyday life. Family influences remained unspoken and unwitnessed. I picked up many silent messages. Mummy's personal life was mostly a mystery to me.

Mummy liked telling me stories of her childhood in a special voice. I was eager to listen, both interested and glad to be with her.

'My parents quarrelled all the time,' she said. 'I wanted to get away from home. One day I told my mother that the headmistress had suggested that I should sit the scholarship entrance exam for Red Maids School.' Nannie was sceptical of her chances but said, 'Well, if the head thinks so, you can sit the exam.' Mummy then went to the headmistress and told her, 'My mother wants me to take the entrance exam for Red Maids.' The head was also doubtful, but agreed because Margaret's mother requested this.

Mummy envied local children who were given bread and dripping to eat. One day she asked 'May I share a piece too?' and received bread and lard. Nannie made her eat it, 'You asked for it.'

There was an innocent recitation to visitors which led to disgrace. 'Recite a poem, Margaret.'

> 'I took my girl to the football match
> To see if she could play,
> She kicked the ball
> Up the nannie goat's hole,
> And then she ran away.'

Despite lack of encouragement Mummy won a scholarship to Red Maids and left home. 'My mother never wrote to me at school. Dad told me once, "Your mother does love you in her own way". I knew he was wrong.'

Mummy was high-spirited at school, enjoying some of her time there. One evening she was dancing in the dormitory and kicked off her shoe. It flew through a skylight, landing in a room where prefects were meeting. This seemed daring to me.

All these stories were strands in the family puzzle. I became closely attuned to my mother, and to her needs in her changing moods. This did not help me express my own feelings or receive the attention which I needed for myself.

There was Nannie, pouring tea-leaves into a saucer and telling us the meaning which she saw there. She turned the cup upside down, reversing it quickly. Patterns remained, traced in tea-leaves; a flock of birds; a scatter of letters awaiting the postman; a dark-haired man waiting to cross the sea and bring good fortune, or find it; sometimes animals appeared. I was absorbed when Nannie read the tea cup. I stood beside her and watched intently.

One day when I visited Nannie she told me about a new lodger in the house. 'She put the radio on the table. Then she said this is a wireless, so it should not have wires. She pulled all the wires out of the radio, so of course it will not work now!'

There was a special Christmas at Cotham Road when we were all together. My great Aunt Rosie came for the first time, a link with our great grandparents, her mother and father, Emily Rose and James White. I knew Rosie was a singer and dancer. Mummy, as a child, loved to visit the theatre when Rosie was performing. Once she belonged to a troupe of young dancers called the Royal Gypsy Children. Auntie Rosie became President of The Variety Artistes Guild and knew Marie Lloyd and other music-hall singers. Rosie was kind, had a lovely smile and a mass of corkscrew curls.

Now she played the piano as we gathered around for a singsong, and encouraged me to sing a solo. There was much laughter, a deep connection with the past, and a feeling of warmth and friendliness as everyone shared Christmas happiness. A man called Uncle Bub appeared for the first and last time. Probably he was a brother of Nannie's.

We did not see Auntie Rosie again until the 1960s when she joined us for Christmas in Chelsea. Mother was very fond of her, so I do not understand why there was so little contact.

Mary Rose White. Born 5/1/1883. Died 5/12/1965. Stage name Irene Rose. President of Variety Artistes Guild. Married George Jennings, who died, then Fred Fitzgerald.

Auntie Nancy Davies, circa 1930, wearing new raincoat bought by Auntie Cass, Eleanor's sister, the cook.

Grandfather James Davies, conductor with Bristol Fire Service Band, August 1944.

Father Glyn Davies with his band, Isle of Wight.

Glyn Davies, 1939.

Grandmother Nina Mary White, with mother Margaret Rose, 1921.

Margaret White, about eleven years old, in Red Maids School uniform, 1931. School founded by merchant John Whitson in 1634 for 'poor women children'.

Margaret White, circa 1930, about ten years old.

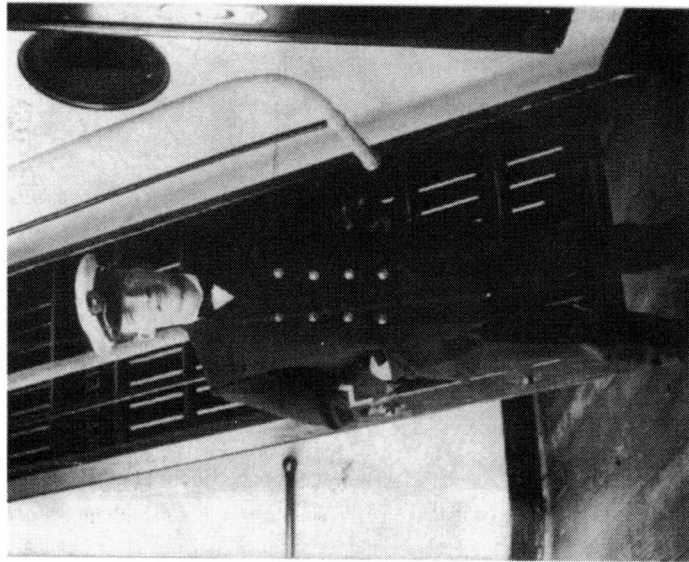

Mother, 1943.

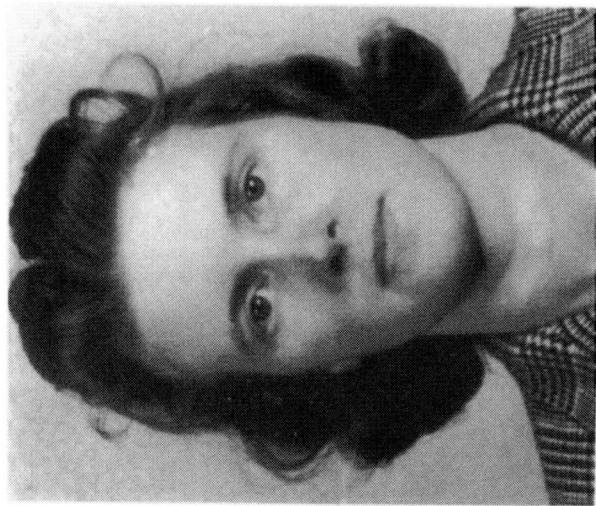

Grandfather Robert White, Purser, 1930s.

Peter and the author, before we went to Nailsea, 1943.

Peter (two years), Carolyn (baby) and the author (four years) with mother Margaret, after return from Nailsea, 1944.

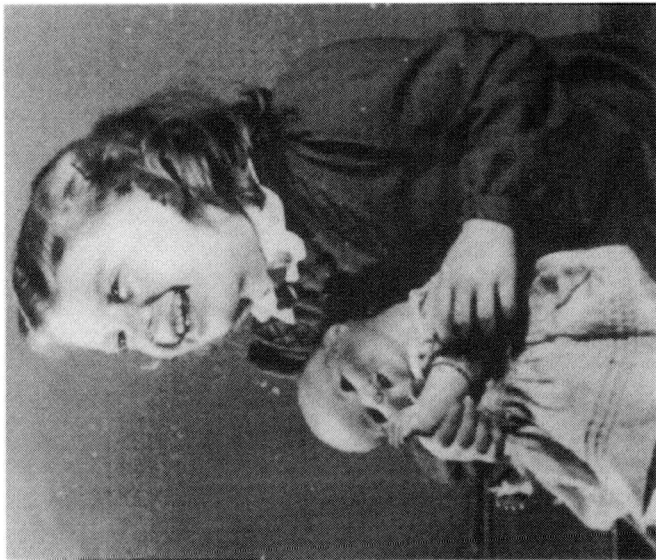

The author aged seven with new red dress. Knoll Lodge, Bournemouth.

The author (seven), Peter (five) and Carolyn (two), Bournemouth, 1947.

The author aged twelve, Cotham Rd.
Photograph by Uncle Jimmy.

Peter (seven), the author (nine) and Carolyn (five).
Trelawney Rd.

Chapter Seventeen

Finding Roots

How did Mother manage to keep a roof over our heads? We moved house regularly, yet there was always somewhere for the family to live.

It was 1948. Our house at 9 Clyde Park in Redland had a friendly atmosphere, and the rooms were light and spacious. Probably this stage coincided with a happier period in Mother's life. Clyde Park was our home.

Mother provided lodgings with breakfast and evening meal for two or three black students studying at the university. In the 1940s in Bristol, racism was more prevalent than now, but Mother was more interested in meeting students from overseas, attracted by other cultures. At one time Mr and Mrs Nawawy and their baby stayed with us, the Egyptians who were already Mother's friends. We also met Nigerian and Sudanese men who came as students.

Mr Fayiga was Nigerian. He was friendly, laughed often and played jazz music in his room. I was intrigued by the fact that he used a wooden toothbrush.

Mr Bukhari came from a wealthy family in Sudan. He was courteous, serious, quietly spoken and dignified, and taught at Merrywood Grammar School. It is not surprising that he became a diplomat in later years. There was a distant yet sympathetic rapport between us. Carolyn called him 'my lovely black man,' and liked to sit on his lap.

Returning from school one day, I saw a small group of children running away from Mr Bukhari, up Clyde Park, with mock screams of fright. Now I stood on firm ground, sure of my position. 'You are silly,' I told them. 'Pretending to be scared. He lives here.' 'Silly yourself,' one of the girls jeered, yet they stopped screaming and walked away.

Mr Bukhari must have been aware of me. Many years later he told Mother, 'I wondered if Maxine would become a nun. She was so serene and reflective.' In those days my energy was turned inwards. I was often reading, losing myself in the world of books. Nannie gave me a bible for Christmas. The coloured pictures, including Joseph and his brothers, and Daniel in the lions' den made a deep spiritual impression on me.

'I'm going to read the Bible all the way through,' I announced. 'You won't be able to do that,' Uncle Jimmy said. He was right. I stopped after a few chapters of Genesis, bemused by the string of names, the begats, yet still the ancient history spoke to me.

I watched on television a vast crowd gathered to celebrate the founding of the State of Israel in Jerusalem. Although I did not fully understand the significance of this event, I recognised that these people were joyful because they had a land of their own. The history and a sense of belonging reached me in a way beyond words.

Mummy bought a box of second-hand books for me from Mrs Jenkins, a neighbour in Cotham Vale. For weeks I read from my own library, ranging from Enid Blyton to Harriet Beecher Stowe's *Uncle Tom's Cabin*. I enjoyed the unravelling of mysteries and accounts of delicious meals in the *Secret Seven* books, usually tasty picnics with fresh bread and apple pie and cream. Girls who behaved badly at Blyton's *Mallory Towers* attracted me, like Arabella who was rude whenever she felt like it, saying things which others found outrageous.

Uncle Tom's Cabin with its poignant story of slavery made a deep and irrevocable impression on me. My heart stung with indignation as I read of terrible ill-treatment, lashings and oppression. Uncle Tom's forbearance and fortitude in the face of hardship stirred my compassion beyond words as no other account has done. Then there was little Eva with her baby, trying to escape to safety over the frozen lake. I was appalled in my awareness of slavery and indignant at such grave injustice, yet I did not speak of this. At home we talked only of essential matters, like when Mummy wanted me to go and buy the bread, or another errand to Mrs Bartlett at the dairy in Chandos Road.

The other book which influenced me profoundly was *The Secret Garden*, by Frances Hodgson Burnett. The story of Mary, the orphaned child who travelled from India to live in her widowed uncle's home on the Yorkshire Moors. The lonely little girl who was befriended by Dickon, and discovered a hidden garden, stirred my imagination. Mary brings back to life the neglected and overgrown garden. Finally her disabled cousin, Colin, is returned fully to health. The story ends with the sad uncle reunited happily with Mary and Colin as they walk through the newly-alive garden. This story focused my dreams in a powerful way – growing, healing, influencing reconciliation – a happy ending to unpromising and sad circumstances.

Uncle Jimmy was teaching maths to children at Cotham Grammar School. He had been a pupil there himself. One day he gave me a copy of Lewis Carroll's *Through the Looking Glass*. The cover illustration shows Alice kneeling on the mantelpiece, seeking a place on the other side of the mirror. This picture evoked a deeper impression than the make-believe world of the story. Gran Davies had given me *Alice in Wonderland*. I enjoyed the beginning where Alice, in search of adventure, fell down a rabbit hole to find a new world. Now the idea of Alice going through the mirror to discover another world, meant more to me than *Tweedledum and Tweedledee*, or *The Walrus and Carpenter*.

Here is a little girl of Victorian days – the book was first published in 1872. The mirror looks like the glass in Nannie's sitting room. There is a bobbled fringe all around the mantel. A clock and a vase of flowers are covered with glass cases. All evoke an atmosphere reminding me of the West Park days when there was time stretching behind our own everyday lives.

> 'A Tale begun in other days
> When Summer suns were glowing
> A simple chime, that served to Time
> The rhythm of our rowing –
> Whose echoes live in memory yet
> Though envious years would say
> "Forget".'

Comics were delivered weekly for us. I read the *School Friend* and *Girls' Crystal*. Peter had the *Dandy* and *Beano* while Carolyn had *Robin*. The arrival of these brightly coloured comics with ongoing tales of School, Desperate Dan and Dennis the Menace was very nurturing. I looked forward eagerly to the thump as the bundle of comics landed on the mat.

Mrs Boyd, our neighbour, lent me her collection of *William* books by Richmal Crompton. I loved William; always in trouble, endlessly inventive. Scruffy, lovable William, rather like Peter, involved in a series of adventures which absorbed and fascinated me. There was Violet Elizabeth who lisped with a 'th' 'I will scream and scream until I am sick!' and all the members of William's family orbiting around him as he concocted fresh schemes.

The Prince and the Pauper was another of Mrs Boyd's books which magnetised me. The idea of exchanging roles was powerful – the prince experiences the life of poverty, the pauper lives in a royal palace. The place where opposites meet.

I loved the story of Heidi, the little girl from another country where German was spoken. Heidi lived with her grandfather in the mountains. She, too, was separated from home, was homesick in the city until she became ill and began sleep-walking. The Edelweiss mountains, the sound of goat bells, Heidi's wanderings with her friend Peter, the goatherd, captivated me, seeming to remind me of a far-off land I once knew.

Many years later, on a visit to Austria, I met some children walking in the mountains, heard the cowbells, and had the same feeling of recognition. This association I link with experience of my ancestors, though whether any of them came from Austria or Poland I cannot be sure. I believe one line of ancestors spoke German.

To and fro I walked to the library in Whiteladies Road. An elderly woman stopped me one day, pointing to the pile of books under my arm. 'You'll wear out your eyes if you keep reading so much!' she admonished me.

'This book was super,' I told the librarian. 'A book cannot be described as super,' she replied briefly. End of conversation. I enjoyed so much visiting the library, hunting around the shelves eagerly. 'Try Angela Brazil,' suggested Mother once, nostalgically, 'I loved her school stories.' Yet Angela Brazil's stories did not speak to me. Occasionally, if there were more books available than my tickets allowed I tried hiding one at the back of the shelf. They were always gone by the next visit.

Carolyn and I enjoyed, more than anything, playing libraries. We stuck little dockets and pages for stamping dates on the title pages of some books at home. There was a date stamp in the printing set I had acquired from Woolworth's. 'You can borrow this for three weeks,' said

Carolyn firmly, stamping in the date. We created a private and cosy world with our books, glue and scraps of paper.

On Saturday mornings Peter and I often went to the Whiteladies cinema, paying sixpence each for the ABC Minors programme. I remember more of the atmosphere in the cinema than of the films. The place full of children twittering like a vast flock of starlings; much banging of seats until the programme began; mock battles and an occasional earnest fight; crunching and crackling of chocolate wrappers underfoot and rustling of popcorn bags. The children sitting downstairs were watchful of the audience in the balcony, dropping chewing gum on unsuspecting heads below. Those sitting in the row behind were inclined to kick the seats in front of them, especially if bored by the film. Cowboy films and cartoons were the most popular.

I met a boy named Clifford at Saturday morning pictures when I was nine years old. We caught a bus up to the Downs after the programme. Somewhere near the White Tree he draped his raincoat around his shoulders, fastening it at the neck with one button. I thought that this was the most dashing arrangement I'd ever seen. 'You're the nicest boy I've ever met,' I told Clifford. He smiled modestly and whirled around like Superman.

Chapter Eighteen

I'll Take You Home Kathleen

Looking back, I see that my Irish great grandfather, Tom Stack, from Kerry influenced our lives profoundly, yet this link and connection with Ireland was never acknowledged or understood.

Nannie mentioned her father only once to me. Mother met him, and much later in life told me that 'He sat in a corner and nobody spoke to him'. 'Did Nannie choose to name my aunt, Eileen, because it was an Irish name?' 'Oh no,' said Mother, 'she just liked the name.'

I found a book which I liked called *The Tinker's Donkey* by Eileen Lynch. The stories of the tinker's travels, linked with animals and Ireland satisfied me, even magnetised me. Reading this tale I felt that I had once travelled with the tinker, recognising the old grassy track we had followed.

The Boyds, our next door neighbours, arranged for an Irish girl, Kathleen, to come to England and help look after their sons, Nicholas and Matthew. Kathleen was in her teens and seemed very grown-up. Her pet name was Kallie. She was friendly and warm-hearted, laughed easily and liked to tease. Often I visited her next door, especially when the Boyds went out and she needed company. Kathleen liked talking of her family and life in Ireland. She also hinted at sexuality, far beyond my awareness at nine years old.

'Once I was climbing a wall,' she said. 'I slipped and a spike on the gate went right up there. You know…?' She pointed with great significance upwards between her legs, laughing at my innocence and her own embarrassment. The pain of the injury made most impact on me; I barely understood the veiled hints around a forbidden zone.

Kathleen said her prayers at night, kneeling with bare feet beside her bed, saying very fast touching words about the Lamb of God, 'And now I lay me down to sleep.' She liked saying her prayers in my presence. I felt safe sometimes with Kathleen.

Once Kathleen took me into the bathroom with her while she had a bath. I felt shy seeing her naked body and large breasts. In our house nobody walked around without clothes on. I knew that it was rude to look at people when they were naked. The wish to be with Kathleen was stronger than my embarrassment and guilt. After that, being naked seemed more natural than before. Kathleen was more at ease with her body than I was with mine.

Sometimes Mrs Boyd invited Peter and me to tea with Nicholas. She was a good neighbour, helping out when Mother once went into hospital for two days. We learned to play *Snakes and Ladders* and *Ludo* as the Boyds had several board games, discovering how to ascend ladders and slither down snakes, vigorously shaking the dice and moving our coloured counters around the board towards home, in the marked out squares.

At home Mummy played records about Ireland.

'I'll take you home again, Kathleen,
The roses all have left your cheeks,
I've watched them fade away and now
Your voice is sad when you speak,
And tears stand in your lovely eyes.'

The real Kathleen next door I loved. Kallie was a living link with an Ireland which nobody realised had any connection with our own family.

When Kathleen became engaged to be married I wrote a poem for her, wishing her happiness when she left for her new home, leaving an empty space next door.

> 'O Danny Boy
> The pipes and drums
> Are calling…'

There were sad songs on some of Mummy's records. Another one longed for the swallows to return.

> 'When the swallows come back to Capistrano
> That's the Day
> I know that you'll
> Come back to me.
> All the mission bells will ring
> The choir boys will sing…
> When the swallows
> Come back.'

Who did Mummy remember and miss when she played the Swallows' Song? Would he ever come back to her?

Chapter Nineteen

Where is Margaret?

We returned from school in the rain. 'Our shoes and socks were wet this morning. Miss Edmunds told us to take them off,' I informed Mummy. 'Let's have a look at what Miss Edmunds saw,' said my mother humorously, laughing with her friend Lilian. I was wearing thick, brown woollen socks with darns in them; maybe Nannie had mended them. At least there were no holes, but the socks were not ideal for inspection by a teacher. 'Your feet are not too bad,' said Mummy, 'but you'd better have a bath tonight.'

We bathed regularly, but usually washed ourselves. Tonight we were supervised by Mummy who came in and out of the bathroom to ensure that we washed our feet – daily life was erratic and unpredictable! Peter floated in the bath creating a cover of soapsuds over his body. A pile of discarded dirty clothes was heaped up on the landing, outside the bathroom.

Mummy often went out in the evening, leaving me to look after the younger children if we were in between mothers' helps. That evening Peter complained, 'I've got tummy ache.' Feeling scared in case his pain was serious, I telephoned Nannie. 'Mummy's out and Peter has a tummy ache. What shall I do?' Nannie said, 'Tell him to lie down on his bed, and phone me if the pain gets worse.'

Next day Mummy spoke to me. 'You told Nannie I was out yesterday. Now she's cross with me.' Life was sometimes confusing! Mummy was annoyed that I had tried to get help for Peter.

Sums just would not work out for me. My arithmetic homework seemed an obstacle which I could not overcome. Unusually, I went in search of Mummy. A smell of baked beans wafted towards me from the kitchen. Mummy was busy, in the middle of serving the lodgers' supper. We met in the hall; she was carrying a vegetable dish in each hand. 'Mummy, can you help me with my sums?' I pleaded. 'How can I do that now?' she asked impatiently. Brushing me aside she hurried into the dining room.

I stood in the hall. A feeling of despair and hopelessness like a black cloud enveloped me. Through the door I stared longingly at the empty sofa. Once, when the liver which I had been given for supper was too tough to chew, I dropped it behind that sofa. There was conflict with Mummy over eating meat which I disliked, especially fat and gristle. Mummy never mentioned the liver, so either the cats obligingly ate it, or we moved house again before the liver was found. Today there was no answer to my problem. I did not ask for help again.

Uncle Jimmy later rescued me from my arithmetic dilemma; he invented pages of long additions for me to complete. 'I'll give you a farthing for every sum you get right,' he promised. Sums became more enjoyable when Jimmy took an interest in my progress, even offering a reward. My arithmetic improved.

Jimmy tried to teach me to ride a bicycle. I wobbled up Woodfield Road when he let go of the bike, yet never learned to ride the bike on my own. I was too afraid of falling, of crashing to the ground.

I tried skipping. Standing on the crazy paving of the front path I enjoyed jumping, holding the handles of my skipping rope. After two or three skips the rope tangled under my feet. I could not skip fast with the free-flowing movement which other girls in the road had achieved.

Looking back it is hard to find my mother. Mummy comes and goes, emerging with certain incidents. Often, it seems, she was not in the house. Usually I was unaware of what was happening in her life, or indeed in our own.

Sometimes there was a mother's help to look after us. A German *au pair* girl, Gisela, stayed temporarily, spanning a Christmas, telling us kindly of the fir tree and decorations which her family had at home in Germany, as we decorated our own Christmas tree together, with silver tinsel.

Peter and I had rabbits. My white rabbit was called Snowy. Peter's was a sleek black one, named Blackie. I looked after the rabbits, feeding them carrots and lettuce and changing their straw beds. It was worrying that Snowy and Blackie had to live in a hutch outside where it was cold. In winter these poor rabbits died suddenly and a neighbour reported us to the RSPCA. This grieves me more now that I understand the implications. The rabbits did not have enough bedding and their diet was probably inadequate.

It was Gisela who broke the news that Snowy and Blackie had died. Dimly I understood that the rabbits were cold and unhappy. Even though I was sad, it was a relief not to see them crouched in their bare hutches outside the house. I had tried hard to look after them. Now the worrying was over, the hutches were empty.

Mummy was often out, only appearing mostly when I had done something wrong. She sent me on errands, usually to buy bread. On the way home I picked off tasty pieces of crust to eat. She did not notice. Most of our shopping was delivered in cardboard cartons by the grocer and greengrocer.

One day Mummy called me into the dining room. 'I need some money. Go round to the Post Office and take the money out of your account.' There were about seven pounds which I had carefully hoarded and saved, and I was reluctant to withdraw my savings. Mummy was cross and insistent. Probably she considered that most of the money came from her in the first place. The Post Office was just around the corner, in Chandos Road, a short walk through the churchyard of St Saviour's. As I walked through I was fascinated by the voices of children in the Church School, chanting their tables, learning by heart. As they progressed with the numbers their voices took on a natural sense of rhythm which propelled them towards a triumphant conclusion.

> 'Once seven is seven
> Two sevens are fourteen
> Three sevens are twenty-one
> Four sevens are twenty-eight.'

I wished that I was inside the school room. The children sounded happy, even eager, chanting their tables. Their teacher called out instructions in a loud voice, 'Now take out your arithmetic books.'

Mother did not return the money. I began saving again.

After breakfast one morning the water heater in the kitchen exploded. The ash penetrated Mother's eyes. She came into the sitting room with a towel held over her face. Very soon, a woman police constable came to the house to stay with us while Mummy was at the Infirmary receiving treatment.

The constable was kind and attentive. She sat with us in the large front room. Talking about school and books I was reading. It was exciting, being looked after and receiving so much attention. Mummy's eyes were hurt, yet more important to me right now was that this kind woman was so interested in me. Wondering how long she would stay, I was disappointed when Mummy returned so soon.

Fortunately her eyes were undamaged. The policewoman went away, and life went on as usual until Joan arrived.

Joan was my favourite mother's help. She had a soft, blue angora-wool fluffy jumper that was so cuddly. Joan came from the north and she had a boyfriend.

I was fond of Joan. At night, sleeping alone again after sharing a bed with Peter, I was lonely. I longed for a cuddle. One night I went to Joan. I was surprised to find that she welcomed me to share her double bed in the small room which was once a kitchen. Sinking into the bed I felt so cosy and secure with the warmth of Joan's body radiating around me. I drifted off to sleep.

Sometimes I lay awake waiting for her to come home, when she was out somewhere with her boyfriend. Joan often brought me back a packet of crisps from the pub. She called them 'crips'. When she slipped into bed, cheerful after an evening with her man, I felt a new security, munching my 'crips'.

I discovered that Joan had periods. Sometimes she left big red patches on the sheet. This was a natural part of the life of her body, part of the intimacy of sharing her bed. Mummy had not explained to me about periods. Joan just said 'I've got my period. Now I'll change the sheet.'

'How are babies born?' I asked Mummy, after wondering for some time. Mummy kept her eyes on the frying pan. 'I'll tell you when you are twelve,' she said firmly. 'You have a special opening in your body.' It seemed too long to wait until my twelfth birthday to find out about being born. After careful reflection I decided that babies must come out of the tummy button: I could not think of another suitable opening.

Every week a clinic for mothers and babies was held in Ashgrove Road. I went along several times, talking to the women and watching their babies. Each mother undressed her infant, placing the garments in an enamel bowl beside the wooden chair. A busy atmosphere prevailed, with people coming and going, small children wandering around, and babies crying. Nurse presided, placing the baby on scales for weighing. The babies were all shapes and sizes, new-borns up to toddlers. They did not like being undressed. Some of them jumped when Nurse weighed them, startled by the movement of the scales, and their little arms waved in protest.

'What is your baby's name?' I asked one of the mothers. 'Joanna,' she replied with a smile. 'How old is she?' I asked, watching as her pink knitted coat was removed. 'Three months,' said the woman proudly, holding Joanna over her shoulder. She tenderly kissed her baby's head. 'Do you come here every week?' I enquired, wondering if I would meet them again. 'Yes,' said Joanna's mother, 'I like to have her weighed and know that she is growing.'

I walked around, attaching myself to different mothers, talking about their babies. Nobody challenged me, assuming that I was with my mother. The relationship between the women and their infants drew me. I tried to become part of this bond by taking an interest in the clinic babies, becoming a helper, passing napkins and picking up dropped booties, just as I had done with Mummy.

One day Joan took Peter and me to the zoo where she met her boyfriend. After a short tour of the monkeys and animals near the Monkey Temple, we sat on the grass. Soon the loving pair lay down together, kissing and cuddling. Peter and I amused ourselves by filling their shoes with grass, then covering them with a green carpet.

Kissing and cuddling was beyond our experience. Nobody hugged or kissed at home. Was I jealous? When we arrived home I seized the opportunity to gain attention from Mummy by talking about Joan and the boyfriend lying down on the grass in such a funny way. Unexpectedly though, Mummy just sacked Joan. Poor Joan was not given another chance, just like our other mother's helps who never stayed long. Usually they were off after a few weeks or months.

I was sad when Joan left. Unwittingly I had betrayed her, probably hoping that Mummy would stop the boyfriend coming on future outings. Joan left a warm memory, wrapped around me like her blue angora jumper.

Feeling lost, I tried to attach myself to school friends. There was a girl called Rona, whose very name was magnetic, but her friendship was unattainable. I chose Moira Baird for my best friend. Moira made wonderful playhouses. At Moira's house her mother let her borrow clothes horses, towels, crockery and utensils, anything we wanted to create a lovely and elaborate playhouse.

When Moira came to tea I tried to imitate this absorbing game at home. Mummy was annoyed when clothes horses, plates and basins were taken into the garden. That was the end of playing the way Moira did, inventively with imagination. The friendship also did not last.

When Daddy came home sometimes, he cooked egg and chips for us. This became a favourite meal. The lovely golden yolks were left as long as possible before bursting one side. Then I loved to eat chips dipped into the runny nourishing centre of my egg.

Daddy was not used to squabbles. When we argued he told us to be quiet, the same way Mummy did. We enjoyed listening to a radio programme about a boy called Horace who talked gobbledegook. As no one understood what he said, he could say anything.

Where was Mummy? I began taking packets of jelly crystals from the kitchen cupboard. Peter and I opened tins of thick condensed milk and I divided the milk into two saucers. Then we ate it all at once. Mummy never noticed food missing from the cupboard.

Usually, she did not swear. Once I heard her say, 'Bugger', when a saucepan boiled over. This was very daring. I was impressed.

Peter took one of his school friends to examine my navy school knickers extracted from the laundry basket. Mrs Nawawy, our Egyptian friend, was learning English. 'What you call this?' she asked, pointing to her baby son's penis. 'Peter calls it a twistle,' I said. 'But you can say dick or cock.' Very soon Mummy told me off for teaching such words to Mrs Nawawy, yet I did not know the word 'penis' at that time. It wasn't fair; I sulked.

At school we learned a rhyme which I taught to Peter.

'In days of old
When knights were bold
And paper was not invented.
They wiped their ass
On blades of grass
And went away contented.'

Peter recited this enthusiastically to Mummy who inevitably rebuked me. 'That is rude. Don't repeat it again,' she instructed.

I stole a John Bull printing outfit from Woolworth's and offered to lend it to Peter. 'Give it to me,' he said, 'or I'll tell Mummy.' Reluctantly I handed the set over to him. He soon tired of it and I reclaimed it.

Next time I went to Woolworth's, Carolyn accompanied me. As we went out of the shop I noticed that she was carrying a jigsaw puzzle. 'You can't have that,' I told her. 'It's stealing if you don't pay for it.' I led Carolyn back to the counter and handed over the puzzle. 'My little sister took this by mistake.' The shop assistant smiled kindly and accepted the box, unaware that I had stolen the printing set recently. It was all right for me to take things I needed, yet I could not allow Carolyn to steal from Woolworth's.

In the 1970s I began to research our family history, and discovered that great grandfather James White was a printer. It is strange that Woolworth's actually stands on the site of Lydiard Place, a cul-de-sac where great grandmother Emily lived after James died in 1899. Mother told then of her staying with Emily, as a child of five and of how kind Emily was to her little granddaughter. She remembered a courtyard with a little fountain, and Emily's white cat, Tishie. I was deeply touched that Mother gave a home to a white kitten, remembering Tishie during the last year of her life. Charlie is a handsome cat who now roams in St Andrew's Bristol, a living link with the Victorian age.

At that time I was bullied in a minor way at school. During morning assembly Diana pushed me. I was seen pushing her back and was in trouble. Miss Wilson sent me to the headmistress, Miss Scammell. Why me and not Diana? I cried with fright into a piece of torn flannelette sheet, my handkerchief. At least I had one. Miss Scammell spoke kindly to me, just telling me to behave well at morning prayers in future.

Soon after this, Ann and Rosalind teased me and pushed me against a wall on the way home. I was frightened more than hurt. I screamed, and a passer-by rebuked me for making a noise. They laughed and ran away.

I did not mix well, socially. Occasionally I went to tea with Ann Lane or another school friend. I dreaded parties because they involved the performance of playing games, winning and losing. I feared doing the wrong thing, looking silly, being a loser. With strangers I felt more than ever lost. Once I went to a party organised for Dr Priddie's children, Christian, Angus and Dickon. I was astonished that the family Nanny supervised children going to the toilet. However, there was ice-cream cake afterwards which I enjoyed. This party felt safer than most as we did not have to play games.

I never stayed for school games on Wednesday afternoons. The idea of playing hockey or netball was impossible. At home I was often expected to be quiet and sit still. How could I run shouting around a field? What if I missed the goal?

As I walked to and fro to school the sight of bombed houses, and especially the church on the corner of Redland Park, saddened me. The church was ruined but still standing. The saving grace was the green profusion of bushes and trees which sprang up, growing through the empty windows. The buddleia with its flowering branches eased the scars of war. Bomb craters remained in Bristol for many years after the war and filled me with desolation: a great gap in the earth where once people's homes or shops had been. The spaces were made safe by erecting wooden fences around them. When I looked down into those great holes left by bombs I had a sinking feeling inside me.

The war instilled in me a strong desire to rebuild what had been destroyed. I wanted to restore the broken, empty houses so that people could live there again. The blasting of the church especially grieved me, for often I found refuge in peaceful churches.

Occasionally, I played on a bomb site in Cotham Vale with my friend Denise Rogers. A garden emerged where once a house stood. White convolvulus flowers appeared everywhere, together with golden dandelions. We picked them and used them as food for our dolls' tea parties. Denise had a wonderful collection of tiny pottery, cutlery, even plaster pretend plates of egg and bacon and other meals.

Beyond the desolation, I discovered the strong power of nature to reclaim those war-torn sites, softly carpeting them with rampant green life that covered the gaping wounds in the earth where people's homes, or a beautiful church once stood.

The buddleia grew abundantly on bomb sites, with masses of tiny lilac flowers clustered together in cone shaped sprays. Buddleia was first imported here from China in the late 1800s. It is called the Summer Lilac in its native land, a hardy plant which can live in exposed areas. Here we also call the buddleia the Butterfly bush, as it attracts the peacock, small tortoiseshell, red admiral, large white butterflies and numerous insects.

After the war the buddleia exploded in England. All the major cities of Britain had acres of bomb sites filled with bricks and mortar containing rich sources of calcium for the buddleia which flourished and grew. This special flowering bush created a healing influence throughout our land.

Today I always plant buddleia in my gardens, and rejoice in the renewal of growth and beautiful sprays of purple flowers.

Chapter Twenty
No Place for Jennifer

Suddenly my father returned to England for a visit. I knew that he conducted the band on the Shaw Saville liners, entertaining the passengers. He was a special person, playing his golden trumpet, and I was immensely proud of him. Daddy brought us tins of fruit from South Africa, and some silk scarves for family presents. He gave me a tall walkie-talkie doll who moved her legs stiffly and said 'Mama' if tipped in the right direction.

When Daddy was around I felt happier. I loved and idolised him. He always sent me postcards and letters when he was away travelling and working, and brought gifts on his return at the end of a voyage.

Although my parents were divorced, this made them more friendly, and Daddy stayed in the house. Daddy even played with us and we had fun throwing balloons around. He played the fool, dancing in his pyjamas, and singing. Daddy was a joker.

'The Lord said unto Peter
Come Forth.
He came Fifth
And lost the prize,' he announced.

So Daddy was home. I felt warm and secure inside. Again he cooked egg and chips for us. Dipping my chips into the yolk, I reached the heart of nourishment.

One evening Mummy and Daddy went into the dining room to talk. I knew that Mummy was asking him to help pay our school fees at Amberley House. Mummy wanted us to stay at our good school. It was impossible for her to pay fees for the three of us, so occasionally we had to stay at home until there was money for fees.

I waited outside in the hall, pacing up and down restlessly. The light through the window over the front door shone over the patterns on the carpet. The squares reminded me of Nannie's house. The door opened and Mummy said, 'You will be going to a new school.' I felt my tummy sink down, but did not speak.

Later, I saw Daddy on the stairs. 'Haven't you another dress to wear?' he asked irritably. I kept my dresses clean because I rarely played. Most of my time was spent reading or doing school work, so I was wearing the same light blue dress with dark blue spots all the week. Taken aback, I went into the kitchen and told Mummy, 'Daddy asked me if I have another dress to wear.' I was surprised when Mummy just said quietly, 'Go and change your dress.' I went upstairs and put on my blue school uniform dress with the familiar flower pattern. Only the year before, my uniform had not been ready. I had worn my best silky green flowered dress to school, feeling strange and trying to answer the questions of other girls. Now I wore my school dress at home.

Soon afterwards Daddy left on another voyage to South Africa on his liner.

Mummy loved films and sometimes took us along for company, and these outings were enjoyable. Now she took me to the Whiteladies Cinema to see a film called *No Place for Jennifer*. Jennifer's parents were divorcing and there was nowhere for her to live, so she went to a foster home. The human side of films like these always appealed to me. Sometimes they helped me to make sense of my own experience. Mummy did not explain what was happening to our own family, and this was her way of communicating a problem. Jennifer was upset that her daddy went away, so she went to a clinic for therapy, playing with animals, especially tigers.

When she ran away in London, Jennifer was terrified when a man followed her on to a bomb site. I was scared too, but Jennifer hid and managed to escape. There was nowhere for Jennifer to go, as her mummy had a new boyfriend and her daddy married again. So she went to live with her friend's family, and I was glad she was happy again.

Suddenly we moved from our home at Clyde Park to a cold, rented house. Later on, we returned to Clyde Park: there must have been a problem in making the mortgage payments. Our lives changed overnight, when we left our most rooted home and changed schools at the same time.

The Brown Bird record was broken during the move.

Chapter Twenty-One
Mothers and Babies

We moved to a rented house in Trelawney Road, Cotham, for a few months, until we could return to Clyde Park. The house had a back entrance from the garden in Trelawney Road. The blue front door looked over Hampton Road. A path with railings approached the row of houses on the hill.

There were fleas in the house: they kept hopping on to my white socks. I learned to pick them off and wash them down the sink. Daddy was embarrassed by the fleas when he visited, not realising that I had learned how to deal with them. Mummy found a cleaning lady called Mrs Wicks who sprayed the house.

For some reason Mrs Wicks frightened me – maybe it was her name. She was old, with a bent back and a crackly voice. I thought that she was a witch in disguise. Mrs Wicks crept quietly about the house and I tried to avoid her.

When a local woman came by the house one day and offered Carolyn and me a bag of apples, we accepted them; kindness of this sort did not happen very often. Later, I wondered if the apples were poisoned and was not sure whether to eat them.

The atmosphere at home was very different now from that in Clyde Park. The house was cold and empty. At times I lived in the same state of foggy greyness inside myself which I remember at Nailsea and Nether Hall, not knowing what I was feeling, and not able to share with Mummy anyway.

In my bedroom there was an old grate which was never used to light a fire. It was stuffed with newspaper, and one evening a little mouse appeared there. I liked the mouse, a live little creature making rustling noises in the paper.

In the dressing-table drawer was a bar of Ex-Lax chocolate to relieve constipation, together with other articles not yet sorted following the move. There was also a book by Dr Grantley Read on *Natural Childbirth*.

In the same drawer I found a book called *The Blitz of Bristol*. The dark cover was aglow with orange fire. I knew that this related to a war in a time long ago, yet the fire still seemed to be burning. I remembered bonfires when the war ended, and the taste of crisps salting my mouth.

Mummy went out and bought some lovely, black patent leather ankle-strap shoes and pink socks for Carolyn. The shoes were shiny, and pink was my favourite colour. I wanted some too. Carolyn wore her new shoes. She found the Ex-Lax chocolate and ate it all at once. However, although Mummy was concerned, there was no major reaction to the extra dose.

Mummy told me that when I was little I picked up the telephone and recited nursery rhymes to the telephone operator. I was nine now but I began dialling the operator to pretend that I was a young child. At first the operator laughed indulgently when she heard me reciting *Polly put the kettle on*. However, after a few calls she became suspicious and very soon she told me not to ring again.

I turned to Dr Grantley Read. Sitting on my bed, I looked with deep interest at the diagrams showing babies inside the womb. They were curled up so neatly, and some were standing on their heads, whilst others lay in awkward positions, with an arm or leg thrust forward. The pages were loose. I read some of the text, but it was more comforting to look at the pictures. Grantley Read knew all about mothers and babies and how babies were born.

I soon realised that Mummy disapproved of the book, when I showed it to my friend Jill Turner. 'That book is not for you,' she said. 'It belongs to me.' Still, when she was out, I found plenty of opportunity to read the book, turning often to the pictures of babies still inside their mothers, or on their way out into the world.

We had a white kitten called Lucy. I was fond of her and looked after her. I liked stroking Lucy, and the way she purred. Lucy ran in and out of the garden. Sadly she was knocked over by a car and killed. Her body was covered over with newspaper so that we did not see her when she was dead. Mummy buried her in the garden. Lucy had a stone with her name marked on it; just *LUCY*.

Then Mummy and Lilian danced around the grave singing:

> 'Put your shoes on Lucy
> Don't you know you're in the city
> Put your shoes on Lucy
> You're a big girl now.'

Lucy had a real send-off. She left a little white gap in the house.

Soon afterwards, Mummy took me to the dental hospital in the city centre to have two teeth removed. They sat me in a chair with a bright light above it. A chain was fastened to my mouth so that it would open while I was asleep. The dentist wearing a white coat spoke kindly, whilst Mummy waited outside. The tooth operation happened in a haze. The man held a gas nozzle over my nose, saying, 'Can you count up to ten?' I began counting, and quickly found myself on a kind of dizzy conveyor belt, with air rushing past me. Then it seemed as though I woke up immediately.

'Rinse out your mouth,' said the dentist, and I spat blood into the silver basin.

On the way home I was half asleep. Mummy did not say anything, just took me home in the car. I felt very woozy. Every few minutes a rush of gas returned, making me dizzy. Mummy laid me on her own double bed, which was unusual. Then she went away.

I lay on the bed crying. My mouth was bleeding, and the gas kept returning in waves which frightened me. Our lodger, Mr Bukhari, came in and very gently gave me one of his large handkerchiefs. Now I had something to hold in my hand and to mop up the blood. As I lay there, time stretched endlessly all around me, tracking back into the past like the end of everything.

Chapter Twenty-Two

A Touch of Gold

We were late arriving at St Matthew's, having left Peter at Kingsdown. The school was a vast grey stone building in Southwell Street, with a large playground surrounded by a high wall. After Amberley House, which looked like other large houses in Apsley Road, Kingsdown was enormous.

St Matthew's was a church building, with only two classrooms for girls, being used until accommodation was available at St Michael's School. The children went weekly to Kingsdown for morning assembly, and for physical education classes in the playground.

As Mummy and I walked up a flight of grey stone steps I felt scared. I was new and it was after nine o'clock. The teacher was calling the register. As Mummy turned to leave me there, a wave of desolation and strangeness swept over me like a muffling blanket of fog, like the feeling of being away from home, at Nether Hall.

'What is your name?' asked the woman teacher kindly. I did not know *her* name. In the 1940s Maxine was an unusual name, and I was apprehensive of being the odd one out. Sure enough; 'That's a funny name,' said one girl. I felt strange and funny too, with a sinking feeling in my tummy. I sat at a desk as our teacher finished calling the register, feeling estranged and uncertain of being welcome in this new school.

Later on, I was surprised to be accepted. There were other girls with more unusual names, like Mavis and Velda. Best of all, one pupil told me that her cousin was named Maxine. In those days I often wished for a more ordinary name. Later I liked the name chosen for me by my parents. Soon I settled down, and enjoyed the singing at St Matthew's. As it was a church school we sang a range of hymns and songs, including Welsh traditional melodies like *Watching the Wheat*, which lifted my spirit.

> 'Daisies are our Silver
> Buttercups our Gold
> This is all the treasure
> We can have or hold.
> Raindrops are our diamonds
> And the morning dew...
> God who gave these treasures
> To your children small
> Teach us how to love them
> And grow like them all
> Make us bright as Silver
> Make us good as Gold,
> Warm as summer roses
> Let our hearts unfold.'

(Glanfinlas, Jan Struther)

The class of little girls sang in bright carolling voices, rising above daily squabbles, problems with sums and worries at home.

> 'Glad that I live am I
> That the sky is blue.
> Glad for the country lanes
> And the fall of dew.

After the sun, the rain
After the rain, the sun
This is the way of life
Till the work be done.'

At playtime the girls skipped and joined hands for circle games in the small paved yard. Being unable to skip I became a rope turner.

'There's somebody under the bed
I don't know who it is,
I'm feeling very frightened
And call my Mother in.'

The next girl leapt into the rope which turned continuously, and skipped a few times before we repeated the rhyme.

Soon after joining the school I fell over in the street nearby and cut my knees. I cried in pain and shock, yet was surprised to find that Barbara was comforting me. Kindly she offered the pomegranate carried in her hand. With a pin we picked out and shared the seeds from the pink fleshy fruit. Barbara was a generous girl with a lovely singing voice.

'I want some red roses
For a blue lady
Mr Florist take my order please.
We had a silly quarrel
The other day...'

Barbara sang a popular song on the way to school.

All the girls were friendly. In the other classroom was Margaret, an older girl. Margaret was attracted to me, and the intensity of her attention alarmed me. Whenever the door opened between classes Margaret eagerly waved to me: I was bewildered by her strong attachment, and she followed me around. 'I want a *Baby's Own Annual* for Christmas,' she told me.

That evening Margaret decided to accompany me home to Trelawney Road. I was frightened, puzzled as to how to respond to her limpet-like dependency and friendship. She stood outside our living room, peering in through the window. Obviously she wanted to come in, be one of the family, be invited for tea. My uncertainty and pain in this dilemma was resolved. Uncle Jimmy was visiting us, and he drew the curtains across the window, leaving poor Margaret alone outside the house. It was impossible to invite her inside. What could I say to her? I sensed a blanketed need which almost paralysed me with fear.

Margaret's sister Mary was in my class, often wearing a short-sleeved green jumper. It was easy to talk to Mary. She invited me into her house one day. They were a family of Welsh descent, living in a terraced house off St Michael's Hill. I was fascinated that their mother was firmly the centre of the family. Obviously she worked hard to keep all her children clean and tidy – six sturdy children, and later the baby, Patrick, arrived.

Mary explained about her sister Margaret. 'She is slow. She wants a Baby's Annual!' Their home was orderly, with polished lino on the floor.

Nearby was the ironmonger's shop. Irene and Cynthia Filer were the ironmonger's daughters, attending our school. One night there was a thunderstorm. 'Our Ma hid under the table when the lightning struck,' Irene told me.

We moved back to Clyde Road.

I became aware of other families living in poverty and hardship. The children wore shoes without socks, and in winter their legs were red and sore. The pupils came from a wide range of homes and I learned more from this diversity.

Older girls minded the younger ones, as I did too, like Marlene Peters, who reluctantly walked around with two little sisters Denise and Lynn, in a pushchair. They wore angora-wool cardigans, cried, ate cakes, and accompanied her everywhere.

By this time our classes had moved to St Michael's School behind the church at the bottom of the hill. Our headmistress was Miss Ellen Heath, who was kind but I rarely had contact with her. I now know that she established St Francis Children's Home in Bristol and was involved in projects for children in need. She was organist at St Michael's Church. Ellen Heath was awarded The British Empire Medal for services to young people in Bristol.

At St Michael's I carefully adapted my speech. Gone was the cosy world of St Matthew's. Instead of 'Mummy' I said 'Our Ma', as most of the others did. The Bristol 'L' frequently added to words ending with 'A', turned this into 'Our Mull', which sounded alien to me. Soon a few children scented difference and taunted me on the way home up the hill. 'You went to a posh school, your Mull got a nannie for you.' This was a grand version of our mother's help, Joan. In vain I tried to demote her from the rank of nannie, calling her 'Our Joan'. Our nannie was our grandmother, who often did things for us. After a while most of the children tired of teasing and accepted me.

I was friendly with Sandra Inglis, an intelligent girl with dark rimmed glasses. Sometimes she became fierce. One day there was confrontation in the playground and I hit her with my library book. She snatched the book and threw it over the railings. I was defeated.

A new girl, Maureen, came to school, wearing a navy gymslip and jersey. She was from Dr Barnardo's Home on

Whiteladies Road and I was drawn to her. The Children's Home interested me and I asked her questions. I felt a sympathetic bond with Maureen, as though we had something in common. I was surprised that she did not cry about living at Dr Barnardo's. I talked gently to her in case she missed her Mummy and Daddy. Soon Maureen left, and I hope she returned home.

Each morning, Mummy gave me bus fares to take Peter aged eight, Carolyn who was six and myself on the bus from Clyde Park to school. I started keeping the bus fares sometimes. The bus conductor was so busy that he did not notice. One day someone's mother did though, and admonished me to pay the fares. Reluctantly I did so. I needed the money to build up my account in the Post Office, for some unknown purpose. Saving money gave me a feeling of security and achievement – a nest egg which belonged only to me.

We left the bus at Kingsdown. Some of the children always went into the shop there to buy comics or iced lollies. My ambition now was aimed towards the future, so I did not spend money on sweets or lollies. Occasionally I went to the off-licence in Chandos Road for a bag of broken crisps which were sold at reduced price. The salty taste appealed more to me at that time than the sweetness of chocolate.

Children at St Michael's were more inventive and active than those at Amberley House – they had more scope. At the private school, break times were spent in an orderly way in the play room, drinking milk and talking. There was no playground, and games were played formally each week at a hired playing field.

St Michael's children roamed freely and noisily in their large playground, shouting, screaming, reciting and chanting, fighting and chasing. A repertoire of games appeared rhythmically with changing seasons – hoops and sticks, marbles, skipping and circle games, handstands against the wall. Boys and girls were taught separately, and had independent entrances to school.

This was a rich new world which sometimes overwhelmed me. I tucked my dress into my knickers like the other girls and had a go at handstands against the wall. Even after assiduous practice I just achieved one leg on the wall; gymnastics were definitely not for me.

I bless the teacher at Kingsdown School who understood my fear focused around physical activity. She gave me a ball with which to play something simple that I could achieve, enjoying the experience of play for the first time in school. In the rough and tumble of organised games I took fright, feeling far too vulnerable and exposed to join in as others did. At home I was so carefully controlled that spontaneous expression and movement were risky.

When our teacher, Mrs Roberts, a benevolent even-tempered woman, next announced games I put up my hand saying, 'Please Mrs Roberts, I have to go to the dentist.' 'Very well,' she responded. 'Bring me a note next time.'

Off I went, relieved to avoid the unknown turbulence of games. I arrived for lunch at Nannie's earlier than usual. 'The teachers have a meeting,' I told her. Nannie accepted my story, and bustled around preparing lunch.

Obviously I would not have a dental appointment every week nor would the teachers send us home weekly whilst they had a meeting.

Next PE day I sent Peter on ahead when we reached the Kingsdown bus stop. 'Come on,' I said to Carolyn. 'We're going to the Downs.' At Clifton Downs we walked around, passing time, then sat on a bench watching passers-by and dogs. I took my little sister to a baker's shop, buying her a bun and a cake for lunch, with her school dinner money. I was expected for lunch at Nannie's, so I left Carolyn on the Downs with her bag of cakes, promising to return quickly.

It worried me to leave Carolyn alone on the Downs, yet the fear of being forced to perform in PE was unbridgeable.

I ate lunch at Nannie's, then returned to fetch Carolyn, relieved to find her in the same place, near the shops. As the PE lesson was over, we went to school in the afternoon.

On the following PE day I took Carolyn to the Museum. We wandered around, looking curiously at the stuffed animals and birds, then paid a special visit to Alfred the Gorilla.

'Daddy took us to see Alfred when he lived in the Zoo,' I explained. 'When he died they stuffed him, so we can still come to see him here.' Carolyn was co-operative. She was strong-minded and sometimes had tantrums which even Mummy could not quell. Now she accepted the new programme; possibly the novelty appealed to her. Again, I bought her cakes, and left her with Alfred while I had lunch at Nannie's. If I did not go, Nannie and Mummy would find out that we were not at school.

That evening, Carolyn possibly told Mummy about going to see Alfred. It was Nannie who first talked to me, 'Why didn't you go to school?' What a tangled web indeed! It was impossible to explain the fear I felt, I hardly understood myself. 'I was afraid of being late for school,' I said.

Poor Mummy was chided for not sending us to school in time. Whilst it was true that we were sometimes late, the real reason remained secret. Nobody at school realised that I truanted several times or knew how frightened I was of playing games, performing physically, feeling so alone in the world. Somehow I avoided PE – the timetable changed, and lessons were less frequent.

Another girl in my class, Janet Press, invited me for tea at her home; a terraced house in Horfield Road. There were four children in the family, three now grown-up. Their home offered a family warmth, lacking in our house.

I felt so sad, yet unable to express true feeling locked deep inside me, so I sat in the living room, looking as sad as possible, hoping that someone would understand and love me. Janet's mother noticed my sad face and made me welcome.

One evening I ate supper with Janet's family, and stayed the night. As I had no nightwear Auntie Eileen lent me a pair of pink flowered pyjamas. They were voluminous and hung on my body in a comical way. Jan's mum laughed kindly, so I did not mind. I was comforted sleeping close to Janet in a large bed, hearing her breathing in the darkness.

Jan went to dancing classes. At a local display I watched her dancing the *Sailor's Hornpipe*, the *Can Can* and *Cherry Ripe*. Although I had a natural sense of rhythm, responding to music with enjoyment, I no longer went dancing. Now I admired Janet as the dancer I wished to be – dancing, too, had become unattainable.

A man roaming around St Michael's Hill exposed his penis to two girls on their way to school. A woman police constable came to talk to us, questioning the pupils. There was a mixed atmosphere of revulsion, fear and fascination connecting to my experience with Papa in the lavatory. 'He showed his cock,' said one girl, 'and I ran away.' How clever that she ran away. Why didn't I run from the butcher's boy, and Papa in the upstairs toilet? It puzzled me why this man waited on the hill to expose himself to girls passing by. What for? Why did he have so much time? Yet the forbidden magnetised the children. Police intervention offered some protection, just as the woman constable did when Mummy had the accident with the heater.

Nurse came to examine the children. It was exciting as we left our classroom in the middle of a lesson. The attention was comforting. We lined up in our vests and knickers. Nurse looked at one girl's body and said 'RW', in a clear firm tone. A clerk wrote this down in the pupil's record chart.

Then it was my turn. Nurse undid my plaits and examined my hair carefully, parting it as she went. I knew that she was looking for nits as I had already had them, and the dread of tiny insects creeping over my scalp returned. Happily my head was clean. 'Now go into the next room and see teacher about some clothes,' said Nurse.

The classroom was heaped with second-hand clothes which local people had donated to school for 'the poor children'. A teacher handed me an ugly purple coat with a fur collar, and a navy blue cardigan.

That night, Mummy was indignant that the school should consider her children eligible for clothes donated for children in need. She relented when she saw the school cardigan, which would be useful in my limited wardrobe. 'You can keep that,' she said, 'but take back that dreadful coat. Tell the teacher it does not fit your sister.' 'Mummy,' I asked, 'What is RW?' Mother paused. 'If I tell you, will you promise not to say anything to the other girls?' I nodded. 'Ring Worm,' said Mummy. 'Little red circles on the skin.' I kept the promise, glad that Mummy had answered my question.

We started going to Kingsdown Baths for swimming lessons. I enjoyed splashing about in the water, and initially was keen. Nannie sometimes took us to the Marine Lake at Weston-super-Mare, and had made towelling bathing wraps for us. On these outings she took the brown egg and tomato sandwiches which we loved. We also spent holidays at Bournemouth, enjoying the wide sands and playing in the sea.

So now I asked Mummy one Saturday 'Can I go to the swimming baths with Jill?' My friend, Jill Turner, lived nearby in Woodfield Road. For some reason Mummy did not want me to go, but for once I persisted. 'Please, please let me go!' 'Oh all right,' said Mummy angrily. 'Please yourself and go!' Knowing that she disapproved so much spoiled my pleasure in the water. I had no swimming costume at the time, so had to wear my pants. Maybe Mother realised that this was unsuitable, as my nipples were budding into breasts. Once in the pool I became aware of this. I stood at the bottom of the ladder feeling very exposed in the open space of the pool, self-conscious about my body which was changing, and miserable because Mummy was angry with me.

I acquired a new swimming suit but soon afterwards, as I was trying to swim, a friend of Peter's grabbed my leg and pulled me under the water. It felt as though I was drowning, so I was surprised and relieved to rise choking and spluttering to the surface. Unfortunately this did not reassure me of safety in the water. It made me vigilant, constantly watching to see if anyone who was near me might pull me under the water again. I did not learn to swim well, though I loved being in the water.

At school we began practising for the Eleven-plus exam. After we returned from swimming, Mrs Roberts wrote problems on the blackboard for us to resolve. I did not like arithmetic. However, I liked problem-solving more, especially where people were involved.

If Fred had three baskets of fruit and gave one-and-a-half baskets to Joe, how much fruit could Jim have if Fred kept three-quarters of a basket?

The sums about baths filling with water seemed a waste of time. Surely it was more sensible to bath without worrying how long it took to prepare the water?

However, Jane has ten shillings and sixpence to spend on groceries. Flour is sixpence a pound and she wants to make cakes. Each pound of flour makes so many cakes, so how many cakes can Jane make for her money? This interested me because I like cake.

Our weekly singing lessons continued. We chose our favourite hymns to sing. Instead of songs like *Morning has Broken*, which we sang at St Matthew's, we were now taught English folk songs and traditional songs.

I was captured by the song of the unknown lady.

'There is a lady sweet and kind…
I did but see her passing by
Yet will I love her
Till I die.'

The words and message evoked a haunting picture of a lady long ago. I saw her in a long, flowing dress, leaving a fragrant scent as she passed by. Now she had gone, the singer who glimpsed her only in passage, would surely love her with devotion always. An impression akin to memory surfaced, as though I too once knew the beautiful sweet lady and still loved her. The atmosphere changed when this tune was sung; I felt as though the lady actually passed through the classroom.

St Michael's School had a close link with the church. At festivals there were special services. For Harvest Festival the children brought gifts of food which were distributed to older people in the district. Mummy sent me to Bartlett's grocers in Chandos Road, to buy something for the festival. I chose a tin of pears which reminded me of the fruit Daddy brought from South Africa, yet during the service, when I saw all the baskets of fresh fruit, including piles of apples and green vegetables, a tin didn't seem as good. However, there were lots of tins of baked beans and soup, so maybe people would like tinned pears too.

The church was beautiful with sheaves of wheat, a specially baked loaf, and vases of wonderful chrysanthemums, in purple and gold. The brass shone. We sang the hymns with great enthusiasm.

'We plough the fields, and scatter
The good seed on the land.'

Then, gathering strength, triumphantly swept on

'But it is fed and watered
By God's almighty hand.'

At Christmas there were carols. The infants' class sat at
the front to sing the *Rocking Carol*. It was touching to see
the small children singing so sweetly as they rocked the
Baby Jesus in their arms. I do not remember any child
misbehaving during these services. Somehow we felt that
the church belonged to our school; that the services were
for us; and I found a sense of belonging and safety in the
church, and loved the music and singing there.

Sometimes on Sundays I went to the Church of St
Saviour's. I enjoyed the hymns and liked the peaceful
atmosphere in church. When the collection plate came
round, my contribution was one penny. I went to Sunday
school and collected biblical stamps which were stuck in a
book. The reward was to be included in the Sunday School
Outing, and I achieved the visit to Weston-super-Mare only
once. Unfortunately that day there was a strong wind so we
children could not bathe, and the wind blew sand on to our
packed lunches. Still, we saw the sea!

One day in class I lifted my dress to show the girl next
to me my navy blue knickers. I cannot remember what led
up to this. She laughed, so I flipped up my skirt again. Then
Mrs Roberts was standing in front of our desk, looking
stern. 'What *do* you think you are doing, Maxine Davies!
Stay in after class.' I was apprehensive, realising that Mrs
Roberts was cross with me. I knew that it was rude to show
my knickers in class, but it was also funny and made
someone laugh. A joke – challenging accepted behaviour.

As the others filed out I felt more and more upset. Finally, I sat alone in the room. Mrs Roberts did not risk talking about the subject. Soon she told me, 'Go home now, but never behave like that in class again.'

The Eleven-plus exams were approaching. We began writing compositions in preparation. In class there was a debate, 'Should animals be kept in zoos?' My enthusiasm was fired and I wrote a composition pleading for the freedom of caged animals who like to roam free, even though I liked visiting the zoo, and especially seeing the monkeys. Equally, I was inspired when writing about the life of gypsies. Unfortunately, when the exam day came a subject was set which left me unmoved. I found very little to write about and my composition must have been dull.

There was an oral examination. I went into a small room where a man and a woman sat at a table. 'If the Sun sets in the east,' enquired the man, 'where would it be at midday?' I hadn't a clue where the sun would be at lunch time, or any other time, so this was not a successful meeting. When the exam results were published, I passed Part One and failed Part Two. I was not considered clever enough for Grammar School, and experienced this as a failure.

Somehow my mother managed to find the money to send Carolyn and me back to Amberley House.

Chapter Twenty-Three

The Wishing Well

A wishing well card from Daddy arrived for my eleventh birthday. The well was pictured in deep pink shades, with flowers growing around it.

Daddy glued a typed message for my birthday inside the well of the card, sending his love and kisses. Above the well was a cut-out picture of him playing his trumpet, and the words:

'GLYN DAVIES, HIS TRUMPET AND HIS MUSIC.
Something Gay,
Something Blue,
Something Old,
Something New.'

I loved this card, being so proud of my father. Even Mummy said, once, 'He plays as well as Eddie Calvert. He just isn't famous.' So later on, whenever I heard Eddie Calvert play *O My Papa,* it reminded me of Daddy.

Daddy had his own band. They played to passengers on the luxury liners – P & O, the *Himalaya*, the *Chusan Franconia* of Cunard Line and the *Mauritania* and *Empress of Britain* with Canadian Pacific Line. The one which I remembered most was *Dominion Monarch* of Shaw Saville Line. Also, I knew that Daddy had played at the Waldorf in Cape Town, South Africa.

I kept a blue tin with a picture of Princess Elizabeth on the lid, full of colourful postcards which Daddy sent to me from far-away countries.

When he played at the Dolphin Holiday Camp, Devon, in 1948, Peter and I spent a happy week there with him. We had photographs from the Devon holiday. Daddy wrote below a picture of me, 'My Little Flower.'

So Daddy loved me. I adored and idolised him; he seemed magic in some way. Also I loved and responded to music, and my father lived in a world of music and dreams expressed in so many beautiful songs and themes: Daddy and his golden trumpet.

Now I carried the birthday card to school and proudly showed it to my teacher, Mrs Roberts, and other children. Adapting my speech appropriately I said, 'Our Dad sent this card for my birthday. He plays the trumpet.'

At assembly in Kingsdown School one day, just before moving from St Matthew's to St Michael's School we sang the hymn:

'Eternal Father, strong to save...
...O hear us when we cry to thee
For those in peril on the sea.'

Suddenly I was scared: I knew that Daddy was far away in a ship on the ocean. Fervently I prayed that the liner would not sink. At the back of my mind was the story of the wreck of the Titanic in 1912 when more than 1500 passengers and crew died in this tragedy. Dramatising a picture of my father at sea also was a way of bringing him more alive in his absence, keeping a lifeline going over the miles. I worried often about Daddy; he might be cold or lonely because he had no house in which to live; he lived in a ship on the sea, sailing from one country to another; he kept all his clothes in suitcases. How I wished I could find a warm coat for my daddy.

Soon after this, Daddy returned safely to Bristol and I was delighted and very proud when he met me from school. As nobody ever met me from school, this made more impact on me.

Daddy looked handsome. He was immaculately dressed. His beige raincoat seemed a mantle of protection for me, even though he was the one wearing it. There was a gold ring on his finger which reflected his worth to me. His voice was gentle and musical with a Welsh lilt.

Oh, I was proud that day to be seen with my father. 'This is my Dad,' I told any child who was near us, as we walked along past the railings around the playground. I *belonged* that day: this was my daddy, meeting me from school. We travelled home together on the bus.

Daddy took Peter, Carolyn and me in a cab to have tea with our grandparents who lived at Huyton Road, Fishponds. Eleanor Davies, our Gran, had laid out a special tea for us in the sitting room. We ate peaches and cream for tea, and several different kinds of cake. Gran had a glass-fronted cabinet which fascinated me. Inside were varied pieces of patterned china, little glasses and animals. I stood looking, admiring the Welsh dishes.

Gran talked to Daddy about a recent visit from our cousins; his brother Emrys' children, Julie, Garth and Shirley had been to stay. 'Julie', said Gran, 'invents a dance, a song and a poem every day.' My cousin's achievements were inspiring, stirring my imagination. However, the family lived at Mevagissey in Cornwall with their mother Sadie and Uncle Emrys who was a customs officer, so Julie and I did not meet until I was twenty-one when she came to work in London. My own dancing classes petered out after I was given the part of the donkey in the dancing

display. This seemed an impossible role, and I stopped
going to rehearsals.

Our grand-dad James was very kind to us. He talked in a
gentle way which reminded me of Daddy. That day we also
heard about our Uncle Ken, and Aunties Nancy, Prue and
Eunice, as Gran gave news to my father. We knew Auntie
Nancy and Uncle Dan Lacey as we had played with cousin
Royston when we had tea near Eastville Park. His soft,
buttoned slippers told me that he was loved and looked
after carefully. Grand-dad took us out into the garden to
play. I liked the brown tiled path which was old and made
me feel safe. It was like pictures made of tiny stones. What
was the picture behind the old brown tiled path?

In the 1990s I searched for the names of my Jewish
ancestors, as well as the Welsh family I knew.

I found my great grandfather, Charles Daniel Davies, a
municipal officer and town crier, listed in the 1881 Census
of Maesteg. He lived with his wife Joanna, her sister Esther
Edwards, and first two children, Charles and Rose, born
before my grandfather James in 1893.

When I discovered the marriage of Charles Daniel's
parents, in the records of St Mary's, Whitechapel, London, I
was hopeful of connecting with the Jewish line which I feel
so strongly influencing me. Charles William Davies, a
general dealer of Whitechapel, married Frances Belk on
14th July 1816. However, enquiries through Jewish history
societies and the Court of the Chief Rabbi suggested that
Belk is a well known Yorkshire name. A knife which
belonged to Eleanor Davies was made by G.W. Belk, a
cutler of Sheffield.

Possibly the mother of Frances Belk was Jewish. During
a service in the Liberal Synagogue at Easton, Bristol I was
influenced to receive her name. Many messages have come
to me through the years. The closest I came to the truth
was my dream of the child Rebecca. Alice Walker said,

'Life, ended at a point, always falls backwards into the little that was known of it.'

I thank most dearly Rabbi Hillel Avidan and Ruth his wife, then at Ealing Liberal Synagogue, who received me in love and truth of Jewish ancestry, to celebrate the first Passover Seder of my life, in 1991. A Festival of Freedom.

Long ago, at this season, on such a night as this,
a people – our people – set out on a journey.
All but crushed by their enslavement, they yet
recalled the far-off memory of a happier past.

The Jews have a message of freedom which offers liberation to all people –

'Freedom from bondage
and freedom from oppression
Freedom from hunger
and freedom from want
Freedom from hatred
and freedom from fear
Freedom to think
and freedom to speak
Freedom to learn
and freedom to love
Freedom to hope
and freedom to rejoice;
soon, in our days.'

These are beautiful words from the Passover Haggadah.

BARUCH ADONAI
Praise to God.

After we had explored the old path and garden, Gran and Grand-dad kissed us before we returned home.

Before Daddy left on the next voyage I was invited to stay with Pamela, a friend who lived at Portishead. Daddy took me by car to Pamela's house. He said goodbye soon after we arrived at the door.

Suddenly, inside the large house, which was strange to me, I felt desolate and cold. Daddy was gone. I didn't know Pamela or her mother well.

He had gone! I couldn't remember the goodbye very well. I felt cold, frozen inside myself. I dreaded Daddy going away. I didn't know where he was going, or when I would see him again.

Someone was playing the piano downstairs. I was alone in Pamela's bedroom, unpacking my nightie and washing things. Pamela was singing:

'Some day my prince will come,
Some day I'll find my Love.'

I sat in her empty room on one of the twin beds, crying quietly. Pamela came into the room, 'Why are you crying?' she asked. It was impossible to tell her why, so I said, 'I'm pretending to be a girl in this book I'm reading.' Pamela looked doubtful about this story. Time stood still.

Downstairs I discovered that the family had a television, fairly unusual in 1950. We watched *Muffin the Mule*, presented by Annette Mills. This distracted me from missing my father, and cheered me up.

Daddy sent us a scrap-book which he had made for us about the *Adventures of Rupert Bear*. Every day he cut comic strips out of the newspaper and glued them into a book, so that we could read the whole story. Sometimes I read the book to Peter. He and Carolyn often preferred listening to my reading stories to them, rather than reading for themselves.

Postcards and letters continued to arrive from Daddy, sent from all the countries which he visited. Part of me sometimes felt away at sea with him: looking at the far-away places on the postcards I crossed water in spirit and imagination. Some of the stamps showed beautiful flowers and fruit, far more interesting than most of our English ones showing King George's head. I asked for a stamp album and became an eager stamp collector. Through the bond with my father I linked myself with so many new countries.

A rhyme in a poetry book appealed to me:

> 'I had a little nut tree,
> Nothing would it bear
> But a silver nutmeg
> And a golden pear.
> The King of Spain's daughter
> Came to visit me,
> All for the sake
> Of my little nut tree.
> I skipped over water,
> I danced over sea,
> And all the birds in the air
> Couldn't catch me.'

My friend Joy had a walnut tree in her garden. I loved the boat shape of walnut shells. Inside the shells, nuts curled around the boat.

Where was my mother? One night I was dreaming feverishly, on board a ship. The great boat was rolling about. I had to keep counting. Suddenly I woke up in the night and was seasick over the side of my bed. Mummy came in and cleaned me up in a matter-of-fact way. She was not cross.

Then came an experience which shocked me. I was walking along with another girl on the way to school and we passed the pedestrian crossing at the top of St Michael's Hill. An unpleasantly sweet taste crept into my mouth. The feeling was creeping up on me like cotton wool, with a humming noise inside my ears. My jaws clamped together. I was gripped by a strong force beyond understanding. Mute, I continued walking in a state of terror. No longer myself, I was taken over by the sweet taste, the humming and the fixed paralysis of my jaws.

Gradually the humming receded, my jaws relaxed – I was me again. Feeling very shaken and frightened, with trembling legs, I turned into Southwell Street and walked on to Kingsdown School for assembly.

A few days later I was playing with a snapdragon flower in the garden. The sweet taste returned into my mouth, and the humming to my ears. Although the experience was never as powerful as the first time, minor seizures continued to frighten me.

Nannie decided that my diet was inadequate. She criticised Mummy's efforts to feed us, and prescribed Virol. 'Let her come and have lunch with me,' she said, so each day I walked from school to Nannie's house at Cotham Road. She cooked a lovely lunch for me. This gave me a feeling of safety, and I had no more fits.

Yet I was overtaken by a feeling of total weakness as I sat on the chair, looking at an appetising plate of chicken and vegetables in front of me. I felt faint and frightened and began to cry. 'Now stop that,' said Nannie. 'Pull yourself together.'

> 'If I sit like letter C
> Bent and crooked I will be.

If I sit like letter I
I will grow up to the sky,' she chanted.

As the days passed, I enjoyed my food and recovered. Auntie Eileen came in from work. 'Do you know, Mother,' she said, 'I caught a flea from Cleo. I had to shake out my clothes over the bath.' Cleo was a black cat with a white bib. He liked to sit on Nannie's lap sucking at her waistcoat. She was very indulgent with Cleo.

Auntie Eileen was always kind, and sometimes took me to the hairdresser for a trim. Because she was busy working as a secretary at Parkers' bakery we did not often see her.

They talked about Uncle Jimmy's treatment at Frenchay Hospital. When he was a small boy he put his hand into the fire, burning his fingers, and now he was receiving plastic surgery. I *saw* this little boy putting his hand into white hot flame. The scars on his fingers numbed the pain of the fire burning.

Nannie took me into the cloakroom. 'What a state your hair is in!' She undid my plaits, brushing with strong determination to remove the tangles. I winced, 'Ow!'

Yet it was safer, now that someone seemed to be in charge of what was happening to me.

Chapter Twenty-Four

Somerset House

In 1950 we moved to Somerset House, a large square building in Canynge Road, Clifton. We had a wide garden in which to play and Mummy decided to keep hens. There was also a patch of rhubarb, mostly green, but she managed to make rhubarb crumble for Sunday with the red sticks which we collected in a basket.

I loved the hens, remembering chickens on the farm at Nailsea. We had six hens, and two of them I named Henrietta and Nesta. Unfortunately our hens never laid a single egg. It was enjoyable to watch them scratching and clucking their way around the garden. Then they began to escape, and Peter and I chased them round Canynge Square. They were hard to find; one or two neighbours complained when our hens pecked at plants in their gardens. Very soon the hens disappeared.

We always had cats at home. Peter and I smuggled them into our beds at night, which was not allowed. It was so comforting to have a warm furry body curled up near the pillow. Peter encouraged the cats to burrow down under the bedclothes where they could not be seen by grown-ups.

Sadly one of our kittens fell into a water butt in the garden and drowned: another fell into the lavatory but was rescued swiftly, none the worse for its ducking. Maisie, the tortoiseshell cat, liked to sit on the corner of the bath, patting a furry paw at the drops of water leaking from the tap.

One day our cat, Emma, rushed into the dining-room and ran right up the chimney. I felt scared that she would be trapped. Fortunately we tempted Emma down with some milk, eventually. It turned out that the poor cat had an abscess in her mouth, and the pain had driven her to run away and hide in a safe place. The vet treated her and she soon recovered.

Our bedroom and play room at Somerset House was enormous. The room ran the length of the house, with windows and french doors overlooking the garden, the walls were half-panelled in wood, and there was a parquet floor. Although the room was so spacious it seemed comfortless. Several steps down from the hall divided it from the rest of the house. There was a lavatory with a hand basin in the lobby outside, so we went upstairs only to have a bath.

Carolyn and I shared a bed. The poor child had chilblains on her feet, and at night she sometimes kept me awake, rubbing her itching toes together. It was an uneasy sleeping partnership in the winter, yet sleeping with my sister gave me some warmth and a comforting contact.

As Christmas approached, our mother asked us to come to her room and listen to carols on the radio. We had our tea on a tray, I was surprised by the invitation: it felt that Mummy had suddenly remembered we were her children, and wanted to be with us. A sentimental aura surrounded the occasion, yet the clear musical atmosphere of the carol singing uplifted me, and we were sitting together as a family.

At Christmas I was disappointed to find that Nannie had bought us two pairs of long, grey woollen socks each. No doubt Nannie realised that we needed them for school. However, Mummy bought me a beautiful Victorian doll with a china face, and lovely lace trimmed dress. The doll made a deep impression on me and looked familiar in some way. I named her Clare. I could not cuddle Clare because her limbs were hard and stiff, yet I recognised her as belonging to me. She did not last long in our chaotic household, and was broken when we moved house again.

Every night I took my small, cuddly rubber doll to bed and found her more comforting than Clare. Daddy bought her for me in Bournemouth as a surprise birthday present. I even wished for her when I blew out the seven candles on my cake. I kept changing her name but she did not mind, smiling her way through everything, even when she fell out of bed.

Mummy called me into her room one day and told me to go shopping. I did not want to run the errand and my reluctance showed. Mummy was annoyed, 'Why not go willingly to buy the bread?' she asked. The errand felt like an obstacle, but off I went.

One day she was talking to a friend on the telephone, aware that I was listening. 'Yes, she reads all the problems in *Women's Own*. She thinks I don't know, but of course I do.' It seemed that I should not be reading those letters from women seeking advice about problems with their families. The letters fascinated me. I found the replies reassuring, because there was always an answer to worrying situations which seemed impossible to the writer. The letters also sometimes enlightened me about pregnancy and sex, and how to look after children.

A new wave of mother's helps began to arrive. Daddy gave us a disc he had recorded, singing *Try a Little Tenderness*, so now we could listen to Daddy's voice when he was away.

Jackie was the mother's help who did not like our playing Daddy's song:

'She may be weary
Women do get weary
Wearing the same shabby dress.
And when she's weary
Try a little tenderness.'

Whenever we played the record, Jackie reacted dramatically, running to her room. She begged us not to play the song, but unfortunately this spurred us on to play it more often. Maybe she was recovering from an unhappy love affair, but her stay with us was brief. Did the song drive her away? Or did mother sack her?

Mrs Bickell was a reliable older woman who lived locally. She was stout, wore glasses, and brought a steadying influence into the house. Sometimes she gave us breakfast in bed. Her favourite dish was bread and milk, which to me was inedible. 'Please eat it,' she urged, 'Ivy said you won't touch it.' I so much wanted to help Mrs Bickell in this awkward situation concerning Ivy, who helped with the cleaning, yet I just could not eat bread and milk. Ivy triumphed over Mrs Bickell, but not for long. Someone had substituted margarine for packets of butter in the fridge – Ivy stopped coming.

Then Mrs Bickell left. Mummy found Mary, a northerner living in a Mother and Baby home. Mary Hoult was sensible and very pregnant. When her son, Paul, was born I liked to play with him, and push him up and down in his pram. He was a happy little baby. Paul laughed easily when I talked to him, and rarely cried.

On Sunday evenings Paul kept me company when I listened to hymn singing on the radio. I joined in singing familiar tunes. Paul lay on Mary's bed, his blue eyes fixed on me as I sang *Glorious things of thee are spoken* or *Sing them over again to me.*

Peter and I liked to play on Brandon Hill. Scrambling over grassy slopes we reached a plateau with wide views over Bristol. The city is an inland port surrounded by hills, and Brandon Hill connected me with the historic seafaring past.

I often stood gazing out at the tall buildings and church spires spread out below me in a wide panorama, stretching away towards the skyline. Some of the houses were once the homes of wealthy city merchants.

At the centre of Brandon Hill stands the Cabot Tower, built to commemorate the voyage of John Cabot, an Italian who sailed from Bristol in his wooden ship, *The* Matthew, in 1497, and discovered Newfoundland. This voyage impressed me deeply as we climbed the steep winding steps of the tower for a dizzy outlook from the top.

Many sailors set out from Bristol, including James Dyer, my great grandfather. My grandfather, Robert White, was also a seaman. Recalling how the voyage of John Cabot made an exceptional impression on me, and how I recognised it as meaningful, I now wonder if one of my Dyer ancestors sailed with John Cabot. Certainly there was a sailor named Methuselah Dyer in the 1700s. The Merchant Venturers' records show that 'Rachel Davis was married to Methuselah Dyer, a seaman aboard a man of war.'

In between visits to Brandon Hill Peter spent most of his time roaming the Downs with his friends, and they were befriended by a tramp who talked to them. A teacher from Christchurch School, which Peter and Carolyn attended, became concerned, and she persuaded Peter to join a local church choir. Mummy said that Peter was running wild and should go to boarding school.

She prepared him for the interview at Beaudesert Park near Stroud. 'Don't say you go to Christchurch School – tell them you have a tutor at home.' When Peter was asked

'Where do you go to school now?' he replied, 'Oh, I have a man in!'

It was strange at home without Peter; I missed him when he went off to school. It is a mystery how mother paid the school fees, although periodically, there were crises when fees were unpaid.

Mummy went to London for a weekend to see South Pacific. Mary was left in charge of us. At bed time she tried to give Carolyn medicine without the usual jam afterwards, so Carolyn strongly objected to the way in which Mary managed her and began protesting. Mary took hold of her, intending to bundle her down the few steps which led to our garden room, but they both fell. There was Carolyn, now crying in pain. She was heaved into the bedroom and left on her bed. Next day when Mummy returned the doctor came. Carolyn's leg was broken. She was taken off to Winford Orthopaedic Hospital where she remained, with her leg in traction.

Now I was alone at home with Mummy and Mary. As I lay on the bed I was alarmed by a feeling of floating out of my body. It was as though my spirit hovered above me, looking down at my body on the bed. After a while I recovered the feeling of being back in my body.

I missed my sister, realising my love for her. Regardless of her itching chilblains, she kept me warm at night. We argued together in a way which Peter and I never argued: sometimes we managed two or three days without a disagreement. At the height of closeness we sometimes put our arms around each other as we walked along. We were opposites temperamentally. My sister allowed me to be more the girl I really was, not the girl who tried to be so good, hoping to please her mother.

Mother could be fierce and determined, and had me totally under her control. She would not tolerate even a facial expression of resentment or conflict. 'You look just like Glyn,' she said when I was angry, or 'Take that look off your face!'

Yet Carolyn, born nearly five years later than I, in different circumstances, was treated in another way. When opposed, she too had strong tantrums. Instead of bringing out the Hoover, Mother accepted the need to try a different approach: she sent Carolyn to her room to calm down when she had a tantrum.

So it was important that I could be myself with Carolyn, argue and be cross with her when I was out of tune with life.

For a whole week I looked forward to visiting Carolyn at Winford, ticking off the days. 'Now it's Wednesday; I can see her on Saturday.' Mummy visited her frequently. I felt jealous of the special presents, and even little jellies taken to Carolyn.

Saturday came, and Mummy took me to visit my six year old sister. It was a deep disappointment to find that children were not allowed into the ward in case of infection, so I could only look at Carolyn through the large glass window forming a barrier between us. There she was in bed with her leg suspended in the air. We waved to each other, and tried to talk through the glass.

Soon afterwards, Daddy returned from a voyage to Australia. He brought a bear for Carolyn, which simply became *Koala*, a favourite for years. Carolyn knitted endless scarves for him.

Daddy gave me a black doll dressed in a leopard-skin fur, and wearing bead bracelets. The doll intrigued me. I still took my rubber baby doll, Rosemary, to bed though; her body was soft and I could cuddle her.

At last, the day came when Carolyn came home from Winford. She was taller and her hair had grown longer, but she was not allowed to walk far at first. While in hospital Carolyn was befriended by visitors from the Salvation

Army. They taught songs to the children, so there was a new repertoire of songs to be sung at home:

> 'Joy, Joy, Joy,
> With Joy my heart is singing.
> My sins are all forgiven
> I'm on my way to Heaven,
> My heart is bubbling over
> With its Joy, Joy, Joy.'

We liked the tune and celebratory nature of this song, so we sang it together.

Soon after Carolyn returned home we went for a walk, crossing the Suspension Bridge to Leigh Woods. Carolyn did not like heights and sometimes wanted to lie down on the bridge, so I hurried across. 'Don't look at the view,' I said, feeling a little dizzy with height myself, yet the view was so impressive. A vast perspective of rocks and trees, the River Avon winding its way towards the sea, and cars like Dinkie toys sped along the road far below us. I kept looking ahead, at the trees on the opposite side of the bridge. 'There's the wood, that's where we'll go today.'

When we arrived in Leigh Woods I began searching for bluebells. There were no flowers to be seen, just a clearing, and the density of trees all around us. Now a young man wearing a grey raincoat emerged from the trees. He greeted us in a friendly way, 'Hello there,' and began chatting. 'Have you seen any bluebells?' I asked. 'Yes,' he replied unhesitatingly. 'There are some just through there. Shall I show you?'

Carolyn had walked far enough already and I suggested that she sat down for a rest while I picked bluebells. The friendly man assured us that the flowers were growing very near to the clearing. 'I won't go far. I'll be back quickly,' I told Carolyn.

The man led me through the trees. Very soon I became apprehensive, as there was no sign of bluebells. Carolyn was waiting for me. 'I can't see the bluebells. Is it much farther?' I asked. 'Just through here,' said the man confidently, yet he still led me on through the trees. Now I felt alert. 'I want to go back now,' I said, stopping. 'I must go back to my sister.'

'Well,' said the young man as I turned to retrace my steps, 'I am looking for a little girl who is wearing white knickers because it is Sunday.' This gave me a shock, and I was wearing white knickers. My heart began to thud. I felt lost and frightened. When I began to cry, the man ran off immediately in the other direction. Fortunately, it was only a short distance now to the clearing. I was relieved to find Carolyn. 'He's a nasty man really,' I told her. 'Let's go home.'

I did not tell Mummy about the bluebell man. Aunt Edie had told me that I was too friendly with strangers, that I should not talk to them. It was my fault that I was frightened, looking for bluebells in the wood.

Soon after the bluebell walk I sat at the table in the dining-room, doing my homework. Mummy and Lilian were talking about Peter. I discovered from their conversation that Peter had run away from school and that nobody knew where he was. He had caught a bus from Minchinhampton to Bristol, yet he had not arrived home. 'I expect he'll turn up here soon,' said Mummy, 'unless he's run off to join the circus.'

I worried about Peter. He must be unhappy to run away. He was lost. Where could he be? He might be hungry. Where would he sleep?

After finishing my homework I went to the play room to find a book. The french doors were open, and there was Peter, holding a large bottle of Tizer lemonade. I was relieved to see him home safely. 'Don't tell Mummy I'm hiding here,' he said. Of course, she soon realised that he was at home.

Very soon Peter, dressed in his green striped blazer, was taken off back to school. He was regarded as a hero by other boys because he had run away. Teachers offered him more attention. Tragically, another boy at the school was so desperately unhappy about his separation from home that he hanged himself. This appalling event haunted Peter.

My father returned from abroad, visiting us as usual. He brought a record of *Sparky and the Magic Piano* which played its own keys! 'Sparky,' said the piano, 'I can play anything you want me to play.' Soon I was absorbed, listening to Sparky laughing in delight as the piano played on.

Daddy stayed the night. After their divorce, my parents usually seemed able to keep on friendly terms. Next morning I went into his room. 'Can I come into bed with you?' I asked, wishing to be as close to him as possible, and needing a cuddle. He looked embarrassed. 'No, you'd better not,' he said.

Soon afterwards, Daddy said goodbye again. It was always painful saying goodbye. I stood at the front door, watching him walking up the street. He turned to wave and then he was gone. I began to weep quietly. 'What are you crying after him for?' asked Nannie scornfully. 'He's never done anything for you.' Her response stung me and I felt ashamed of my grief for Daddy going away. Yet I loved Daddy, felt loved by him and although separation was painful, this love helped me to survive.

We moved from Somerset House to stay with Lilian, her husband Steve Bowell and daughter Lindsay, at Christchurch Road. It must have been during school holidays as Peter was there with us too.

Peter and I shared a bedroom at the front of the house. Lilian's house was opposite St Brenda's Maternity Hospital, and at night I was fascinated watching the nurses carrying babies to their mothers for feeding. When the blinds were pulled down, I felt that something was missing; I missed the mothers being there for me to watch from across the road.

One day Mummy told me to take the children to the zoo. We often went there, and I did not want to go again, so I set off with Peter, Carolyn and Lindsay, who was five years old, and I led them to the museum. Instead of seeing live animals, we wandered round the glass cases looking at dead, stuffed creatures. 'That's Alfred!' I told them. We took a special interest in our old friend the gorilla: he was once alive when Daddy took us to the zoo.

I realised that as entry to the museum was free I could keep the zoo entrance money to save in my post office account.

The children were interested in the museum birds, reptiles and animals. However, when we returned to Christchurch Road, they told Mummy that we had not gone to the zoo, 'We went to see Alfred.'

Mummy was cross, yet, as usual, when I did something which seemed really wrong she did not say much about it. The children had been out with me all the afternoon anyway. I felt guilty, and she reclaimed the zoo entrance money.

Lilian prepared the tea. I ate slice after slice of bread and butter until my tummy felt full, and the large plate was empty.

The next time I went to dancing class the teacher gave me a ballet dress on loan to wear for an exam. 'Ask your mother to starch it,' she said. Mummy did attempt to starch the dress, but did not iron it. I was worried about the grey looking limp layers of ballet skirt.

At the school an older pupil was asked to iron my dress for me, so I had to take it off in front of the other children and stand naked except for my pants, until she returned. I felt very exposed, painfully aware that my breasts were tenderly beginning to develop. Crossing my arms I covered my body. The ballet student returned with the dress transformed, now all the tulle stood out around the bodice.

Wearing the dress now gave me confidence as the examination began. 'You have very good elevation,' I was told after some springy jumps. Then I was asked to mime – finding and picking a wild flower. I passed the ballet exam for Grade One, and continued to dance every week.

Chapter Twenty-Five

The Sun, Wind and Rain

Mummy asked me to take Carolyn to her class in Pembroke Road run by the Bristol School of Dancing. In the large Studio room I sat with a few mothers who stayed to watch their children dance. The piano music and ballet dancing magnetised me.

'Step together, step close,' called the teacher in a clear ringing voice. The pianist watched the children, adapting her playing. She waited when the teacher needed time to show the steps.

I remembered early lessons with Miss Maddocks in West Park. 'Could I come to this class?' I asked at the end of the lesson. 'Certainly you can,' smiled the teacher, and Mummy agreed. I was eleven years old. I began to dance with a class of mixed age pupils, and looked forward to the weekly lessons. The earlier training had prepared me to participate easily in this class. I enjoyed dancing best when accompanied by piano music. If the pianist was away, dancing became a series of exercises. 'And, *jeté, jeté, jeté,*' across the room. The dancing school began to prepare pupils for a performance of the Sun, Wind and Rain Ballet at the Theatre Royal.

There was a little girl named Leila in the class – her name reminded me of lilac. Leila's mother accompanied her to class. She stayed to watch her daughter dance, and was obviously a loving and encouraging mother.

Was it Leila who danced the Sun? I was entranced by the Grieg music and outward flowing steps of the dance, especially when the Sun appeared in her golden costume for the dress rehearsal. Carolyn and I were cast as clouds. How I longed to be a Pink Cloud but authority decreed that I should be Grey, whilst my younger sister was chosen as Pink. The little ones were beautiful as Rain Drops with head circlets, clustering together for the tinkling, pattering music.

The Ballet was a profound experience for me, containing such a range of dance, and expression of feeling and music. There were boys who danced lightly, yet with great vigour and strength, as Breezes. One girl danced the Wind, darting across the stage attuned to gusts of music.

It was exciting at the live performance, to dance on the stage of the historic Theatre Royal. I wore a grey off-the-shoulder costume created from a dyed vest converted into a leotard, and my head was covered with a grey fluffy wig. As I glided across the stage, I hoped that my white knickers did not show below the costume. My schoolfriend, Ann, was sitting in the audience. Dancing with so many children offered a sense of belonging: we were dancing together, creating harmony.

One of the Rain Drops cried, stopped in the middle of the pattering and had to be rescued from the stage by her mother.

The Ballet was beautiful, and successfully created the elements of Nature. At the end there was enthusiastic applause from the audience of indulgent parents and friends.

After we returned home I wandered around the garden for a long time, wondering how I could write a play which would be performed at the Theatre Royal. Dancing in this Ballet was the most inspiring experience of my childhood.

I walked around humming music of the Sun, the Wind and the Rain. Even now I still recreate that experience when playing passages of Grieg on the piano.

Chapter Twenty-Six

Room for One More

Our last Bristol home, before moving to London in 1952, was in Clifton. For a short time we lived at Clifton Park Lodge, a large house facing College Road, on the corner of Clifton Park.

This house had a strong eerie atmosphere around the hall and staircase, which filled me with apprehension. The hall was large and the stone staircase curved upwards. The house felt deserted and empty, yet there was an unknown presence. Nothing unusual actually happened there, still I felt nervous, ill at ease. No story emerged to explain this powerful atmosphere: I can only connect this with unknown events of the past.

At night especially, even sharing a bed with Carolyn, I sometimes lay awake, expecting an apparition or unexpected intruder. One night I heard the crunching sound of footsteps on the gravel in the drive outside. The net curtains blew gently in the wind at the open windows. Would a burglar break into the house? Would a ghost appear? Yet still nothing happened.

Years later, Mother told me that Clifton Park Lodge was the only house of so many in which we had lived, where she felt afraid. 'I had to lock my door at night, even though I knew that the children were shut out on the other side.' We never went into Mother's bedroom, yet I understood that she did not want to lock us out. The sinister atmosphere compelled her to protect herself. Was it unresolved experiences of our own ancestors, combined with the atmosphere of the house which haunted us?

At Amberley House on the morning of 6th February 1952 we heard that King George VI was dead. He had died early that morning, in his sleep, at Sandringham.

'We will have a minute's silence in each class to remember King George,' said Miss Scammell. There was a serious atmosphere as we sat quietly at our desks: death was a solemn state which I did not understand. Combined with King George though, it became momentous. On the newsreels at the cinema, I had noticed that he was a kind man, so everyone would be sorry that he was dead.

At tea time Carolyn told us, 'Gordon was sick on his desk during the King's silence.' She paused. 'There was a cherry in the middle!' In her class this event had been more impressive than the death of King George.

One morning at the Lodge Mummy brushed my hair for the first time. 'I have decided to adopt Mrs Ahmed's baby,' she told me. Looking down as she brushed vigorously I noticed her swelling and rounded belly. I was twelve years old, and wondered if Mother was pregnant. She continued referring to Mrs Ahmed whom we had never met.

In December we would all move to London. 'Bristol is very racist,' said Mummy. 'Mrs Ahmed's baby will be accepted more easily in London.'

Suddenly the future was so uncertain. Bristol was my home, where I knew and loved the buildings of soft west country stone. The streets and solid grey pavements I walked were also part of my world. I wished fervently to stay, not to go away from Bristol.

We enjoyed a day at the Marine Lake, Weston-super-Mare. My skin was fair and sensitive and I was burned by the sun. Mummy put calamine lotion on my red shoulders that evening. Although I winced, it was the first time that I could remember her touching my body; the lotion did soothe the pain.

Mummy rented a garden flat in Bournemouth and we spent our last west country summer together there, with Peter home from boarding school. It was obvious that Mummy was gaining weight, yet the fiction of adopting a baby was maintained. She spent more time with us. We were there alone with her and she had no friends in Bournemouth. Our relationship with Mummy had begun to change, due to this pregnancy. Later on, in London, we lived more as a family, in daily contact.

A Siamese cat with a loud plaintive miaow visited us in our flat. We welcomed him, yet he chewed holes in any woollen garment which he found. The cat even ate a hole in the shawl which Mummy was knitting for Mrs Ahmed's baby.

We spent some happy days together on the beach. When the weather was fine Mummy took sandwiches, and we stayed all day on the wide sands. I loved splashing about in the sea. When the tide receded, there were the wonderful rock pools remembered from earlier holidays, crabs and tiny fish to watch, strands of seaweed to pop.

On the beach I made friends with Valerie who once came home for tea. 'Do you know how babies are made?' she asked. We were in my bedroom and the door was open. I knew that Mother was around and that this topic was taboo, so I hedged around the subject as best I could. Even so, when the young girl went home, Mummy tackled me angrily. 'Don't you dare talk to her about sex. She must ask her own mother!' I felt hurt and confused by her angry attitude, especially as she looked pregnant yet talked about adopting a baby.

Mummy took us to the cinema near our former boarding school, Nether Hall. There was a film showing, about a couple who fostered a large number of children; it was called *Room for One More*. I revelled in this story, ever fascinated by large families, human experiences and ways of looking after children.

It was satisfying to see how these children, who all had troubles and problems in their own families, found a new home where they were welcome, and settled down to a new way of life.

As summer ended our lives changed radically. Mummy returned to Bristol, very busy with plans for Mrs Ahmed's baby, due in December. She arranged to stay with her friends, John and Barbara Reardon, and their daughter Shelagh. Mummy also told us that she would be going into hospital for an operation, so this was why we could not remain at home with her.

Peter returned to Beaudesert Park School. Carolyn and I went to stay with Aunt Edie's daughter, Eileen, for three months. Eileen was married to Peter Nelson, a Post Office engineer, and lived at Wraxall, a village near Bristol.

Chapter Twenty-Seven

The Willow

Our new home with Eileen and Peter Nelson was a cottage standing alone in the middle of fields, near the village of Wraxall. Eileen, being Aunt Edie's daughter, had known me since I was three years old and Carolyn since babyhood. The cottage was pleasant, comfortable and spacious. The large living room had windows overlooking the flower and vegetable gardens at the back, and fields, with grazing steers, at the front.

The outside lavatory was at the end of the garden. The wooden seat had a bucket underneath, which was regularly emptied into the cesspit. At night a tin pail was placed in the spare room. We went there if we needed to wee. Eileen exhorted us to do our 'big jobs' during the day.

We used oil lamps. Each night Eileen handed me a small lamp to carry upstairs when we went to bed. The soft light cast shadows, yet created a cosy atmosphere. Carolyn and I shared a double bed with brass rails – possibly the one in which I slept as a small child on Aunt Edie's farm at Nailsea. There was a cotton counterpane with fringed edges.

Eileen fed us well. Physically, she looked after us more carefully than we were accustomed to at home; we were supervised when we washed ourselves, and once a week, a large tin bath was taken off the wall in the kitchen, and then both of us had a thorough soaping in the warm room.

We were given regular nourishing meals, with fresh vegetables from the garden, organised in our activities, and sent off to school in good time, with packed lunches in our tin boxes. We ate thick sandwiches, sometimes with a filling of mashed potato mixed with Bovril, or cheese and pickle or bacon. Usually we had a home-grown apple for lunch too.

Our clothes were carefully washed and ironed. I liked to change my pants daily; I was twelve years old. I was surprised when Eileen said that this was too often – that twice weekly was sufficient. Carolyn was nearing her eighth birthday; she did not care how often she changed her knickers, so I wore the larger of her two allocated pairs, meaning that I could change my pants three times a week!

Peter Nelson was a GPO Engineer. He was easygoing and reliable but left the care of us to his wife. I was sorry to hear that following a motor cycle accident Eileen had miscarried the baby they had been expecting. Later, they created a family of four children. We did not have much contact with Peter but he was a steadying influence in our confusing family circumstances, treating us kindly.

One day a tiny field mouse ran into the cottage. Eileen chased the furry creature up the stairs and killed it with the poker. She was used to country ways all her life, but I found the death of this little creature distressing. It seemed harmless. Why couldn't the mouse be released back into the fields of home? I did not protest, being accustomed to accepting whatever adults decided to do, and being unused to two-way conversations.

Eileen was kind to us. She was more even-tempered than her mother, so a calmer atmosphere prevailed.

At this time of my life I became aware of loneliness which had always surrounded me. Again, we were separated from home. Mother, Nannie, Auntie Eileen and Jimmy and our familiar lives. Neighbours and friends were left behind in Bristol. I could not realise that this autumn passage actually prepared me for leaving Bristol, and my deepest roots in familiar places like Brandon Hill. There we had played, stopping to look out over the wide views of the city nestling below us.

During my first twelve years I gained security from the soft grey and mellow apricot stone of the buildings and walls of the city of Bristol. Lacking a continuous close relationship with my parents, the city became of great significance in giving me roots. I believe that attunement to the very stone around me contributed to the strength which I developed as a person.

So now I began to miss and mourn familiar roads, buildings and open green spaces of the Downs where we played in the 'Dumps', deep caverns overgrown with grass. Even though we travelled to school in Bristol by bus each day, our former way of life had ended. In London I missed even the pavements of Bristol; grey slabbed stone. The songs of Vera Lynn still echoed on the radio. This music connected me again with my early wartime years.

> 'When you are far away
> Forget me not.'

Of course there were the *White Cliffs of Dover*, which I had never actually seen. It was a relief not to miss the cliffs, but the song was still evocative. Vera's voice rang out, it seemed, over great distance, stirring and echoing memories.

We also listened to *The Archers* on the radio, the serial telling a story of everyday country folk. Now I remember only the sound of bleating sheep stuck in a ditch whilst a farmer struggled to rescue them. The relationship dilemmas of *The Archers* engaged me. 'I'm very worried about David,' offered a focus for me, and I wanted to hear what happened when the family sorted out the situations which challenged them continually. Before television was so widely available, the radio was an intimate part of daily life. For me it filled some gaps, staving off the emptiness which sometimes engulfed me, bringing other people into the house, and reducing my sense of exposure to the world.

Each morning Carolyn and I walked across two fields to the road winding through Wraxall village. Close to an ancient oak tree, we waited for the green double-decker bus which arrived at ten to eight to take us to Bristol. Again, I wonder how Mother found the school fees.

One day as I stepped on to the bus Carolyn continued chatting to me. She did not notice the conductor ringing the bell, and the bus pulled away, leaving my little sister behind. I called out to the conductor, who stopped the bus a short distance away. 'Come on Carolyn,' I urged from the platform. However, Carolyn's pride was hurt because the bus had moved off without her, so she refused to get on in full view of all the passengers, including numerous schoolchildren. Reluctantly I alighted from the bus to stay with her. We waited about thirty minutes for the next bus and were late for school that day. This directed attention towards us.

Miss Edmunds questioned me on our current circumstances. 'Mummy is not well. She is going into hospital for an operation soon,' I said, as my mother had instructed me to say. 'We are living with friends in the country until she comes home, and we missed the bus.' I felt sorry for myself, tearful as the story emerged, yet it was a relief to tell a teacher what was happening to us.

Miss Wilson presided over assembly, and played the piano. She was a plump, smartly-dressed woman, pleasant yet unpredictable. I recall her feminine elegance, laced with strong assertiveness and on occasion a stern manner. Miss Wilson aroused apprehension because I did not know when she would suddenly pounce on me for some unforeseen misdeed.

One day she spoke sharply to me after assembly, in front of all the other children. 'Your sister's nails are black, Maxine. What has she been doing – digging potatoes?' There was no reply to offer for such an enquiry. I felt humiliated, standing in the back row, whilst Miss Wilson examined the hands of Carolyn who was at the front with the younger children, wearing a baggy navy cardigan.

I kept my blazer on as much as possible. I was sensitive about my developing breasts and did not want anyone staring at me. I was, at twelve, older than most of my class mates; most of them left for grammar school or changed school when they were eleven. Once, when we were rehearsing a play, a girl named Neva looked curiously at one of the few older pupils and cried out excitedly, 'Oh look, the breast, the breast!' I did not want her or anyone else making such observations about myself.

Before we left Somerset House my Aunt Eileen had come into the bathroom one evening. 'As you are sprouting,' she said kindly, 'I have something very grown up to give you.' She presented me with some scented wipes to use on my face. I absorbed her sympathetic rapport but had no interest in adult cosmetics. Similarly, I was disappointed when presented with a pair of nylons; I much preferred to wear comfortable socks. No way was I ready to move towards being grown-up. Sometimes I longed and yearned to be cuddled, still not realising that it was Mummy and Daddy I needed.

Even when playing tennis, back in the summer, I had felt inhibited from moving about the court, or removing my blazer, regardless of the heat. Now I sat in class, huddled protectively in the navy jacket, struggling to understand decimals and algebra which I disliked and could not comprehend. Occasionally the letters of algebra pleased me, but I could not see the point of moving about all those letters and equations. The problem arithmetic at St Michael's had pleased me and made far more sense. At Amberley House there were no familiar problems with baskets, baths or purchasing food to be resolved.

Miss Dennis, the Deputy Head, still rattled her false teeth around like marbles as she spoke to us. She loved teaching words like miscellaneous, as she attached a label with this word on to a drawer of assorted objects. 'Procrastination is the thief of all time,' she declaimed before beginning an English lesson.

Yet I wrote an essay about a witch in the woods which excited Miss Dennis. She gave me an 'A', complimenting me on this imaginative story. 'It's all bursting out of you,' she said, and I recognised true praise. Within me there was a surge of creativity seeking expression.

On the way home from school we were accustomed to avoiding the steers grazing in the field, although they showed no sign of approaching us. Suddenly there was a goat in the field, which ran up to us, trying to butt Carolyn. For a few days we remained watchful until the goat moved on. I had to coax Carolyn across the field, promising to look out for the goat, and felt nervous myself.

Wraxall was so beautiful in October with colourful autumn changes which I painted in a picture at school. I stuck this to a blotter which I gave to Jimmy for Christmas. All the cattle in the picture are facing in one direction, towards Bristol and a stream runs beyond the cottage garden.

Sometimes at weekends we walked along this stream. The movement of the water, gently flowing onwards, soothed me. The fields were green and lovely, but vastly lonely, with nobody else in sight. There were trees along the bank of the stream and I absorbed their beauty. A willow seemed to reach out to me, with a kind of spiritual sustenance which remained with me: a living presence, with graceful branches flowing down to the water. I stood in the vast open landscape gazing at the willow; the roots were firmly embedded in the Somerset earth; the branches extended towards the great lowering grey sky.

We turned, Carolyn and I, and strolled on along the stream on our solitary walk. A great sense of absence and loneliness suffused me, yet the willow remained in my imagination. I longed for someone or something inexpressible.

On the bus I made friends with two sisters, Rosemarie and Judith Carter who lived in Wraxall and travelled to Clifton High School in Bristol. They wore smart grey uniforms and were carefully nurtured children.

Judy invited me to tea but I had no cardigan to wear except the navy blue uniform woollen which I wore to school. Hastily I wrote to Mummy and back came a five-pound note with which to buy a new cardigan. After school, I went to a shop in Whiteladies Road and bought a fawn cardigan with panels of light and dark blue stripes across the front. Incidentally, Whiteladies Road is named after an order of nuns called the White Ladies because of the white habits which they wore.

I was pleased with my new garment and went off happily to tea with Judy. The Carters' house was well-ordered and furnished attractively. In the kitchen was a washing airer. I marvelled at the row of snow-white socks arranged carefully in pairs. The girls had silver christening mugs with their names engraved in flowing letters – Rosemarie – Judith.

Mrs Carter was politely welcoming. As we ate, she lifted the teapot to pour out the tea. 'What does your father do?' she enquired. 'He is a musician,' I said. 'He plays trumpet and leads his own band on the Dominion Monarch Liner.' 'I see,' said Mrs Carter, still pouring tea. 'Judy tells me you are moving to London. Where are you going to live?' I sensed that the area of London was important to her in terms of class. My mother was snobbish about this too. I was glad to reply, 'Harley Gardens, near the Boltons,' as Mummy had explained. I recognised that this address would pass Mrs Carter's test. Looking back, I think Mother inherited conflict about class and status mixed with the wealthy Stockdales, and a marriage deemed unacceptable.

Mrs Carter must have found me acceptable for her daughters to mix with, as we sometimes went for walks together after that, in the woods and fields. Judy was very agile, and although she wore skirts, was a skilful tree climber. How I admired her for this physical prowess, and for belonging to a real family with an everyday ordered life.

Now, I am able to appreciate the liberal and unconventional qualities of my upbringing which fostered flexibility, versatility and innovation: at that time I craved a mother and father centred family with a predictable home life.

Maybe Judy reminded me too of the Judy Moon of my earlier Nailsea days. I sought her company to assuage the maternal loss and loneliness of which I was still only dimly aware.

One day I asked Eileen if Judy could come to tea at the cottage. Eileen probably recognised a class difference, and was definite in her 'No!' I sunk into a state of misery and depression. 'Here,' said Eileen kindly, handing me a crisp russet-coloured apple. 'Swallow your disappointment with that!'

Judy had become a focus for what I needed at home. Later on, as we were striding through the woods, I told Judy, 'I have a friend called Denise Rogers. I don't see her much now.' Judy shinned cheerfully up a tree, seeing how high she could climb. I began to remember the Rogers family who kept a greengrocers in Cotham Hill. Geraldine,

Denise and Norman whom we met in Cotham Vale: where were they now? What happened to my first real friend, Denise? 'She goes to *La Retraite* School,' I told Judy. Later, in London, I tried to contact Denise by sending a letter to her school. I believe that the Rogers moved away from Bristol, and I waited in vain for a reply.

As we walked along the road, Judy began to sing,

> 'I'm Burlington Bertie,
> I rise at ten-thirty
> And saunter along like a toff.
> I walk down the Strand
> With my gloves on my hand,
> Then I walk down again
> With them off.
> I'm Bert, Bert,
> I haven't a shirt,
> But my people are well off, you know.
> Nearly ev'ryone knows me
> From Smith to Lord Rose'b'ry,
> I'm Burlington Bertie from Bow!'

I enjoyed singing but did not know the words, so could not join in with Judy. I did not realise then that my great Aunt Rosie once sang this song, as Irene Rose, in the London music-halls.

> 'We're a couple of swells,
> We dine at the best hotels.'

she continued vigorously as we walked down the hill.

Very soon afterwards we left for London. My contact with Judy ended, though I wrote to her once or twice. Probably she would have been mystified by the unhappy state into which I was plunged when we first left Bristol.

A letter arrived from Mummy telling us that Mrs Ahmed's baby boy was born on 1st December. She was recovering from her operation at the Homeopathic Hospital and asked us to visit her.

Carolyn and I had not seen Mummy for three months, so were pleased to visit her in hospital. Although I suspected that she was pregnant, I was still surprised to find Mrs Ahmed's baby boy in a crib beside her bed. Apparently, Mrs Ahmed wanted him to be adopted by us immediately. His name was Amir. I was very interested to meet this small olive-skinned baby with dark hair, and pleased that he was my new brother. At the same time, I suspected that he was truly my mother's child. Her story confused me, yet I was glad to have a new baby in the family. I liked babies.

Now I understand that Mother was struggling with racist attitudes, and Nannie's clear disapproval when she knew the truth of her daughter's second marriage. The truth emerged, only with time, and in response to my questioning. I then did not believe that Mother was married until she showed me her marriage certificate. She had married Ahmed Bukhari in the Cardiff Mosque, since he was a Moslem.

Our lives were so separate that we hardly saw Ahmed at Somerset House. Carolyn remembers his leaving. She was swinging on a railing in Canynge Road when he walked off up the street. She was so indignant that he had intended to leave without saying goodbye, and that she spoke to him only by chance.

How did Mother feel when Ahmed's family insisted that he return to the Sudan for an arranged marriage? She was left alone to bring up her son, with us. Ahmed offered to take his son to Sudan with him, but Mother would not part with Amir. Later in London, Amir was given the nickname Nino. This became his name; it seemed to suit him, and was similar to Nina, our grandmother's name.

Nino was educated at the French Lycée in London, mixing with children of international origin. This cosmopolitan experience served him well in developing self confidence. As an adult my brother met his father, visited his family in Sudan and maintained contact with them.

We said goodbye to Mummy by the swing doors at the entrance to the Homeopathic Hospital. I was surprised and pleased when she bent down to kiss us.

This was the first time my mother had kissed me, and also the last time. Her own life was a search for the love which she had lacked as a child, and so she in turn could not give or receive touch with her own children.

This is my last clear memory of being in Bristol, before we moved to London. Out through the swing doors into Bristol, city of living stone, hill views, ships and churches. John Betjeman described Bristol as 'the most beautiful, interesting and distinguished city in England.'

The railway line between Paddington and Temple Meads became our connection with Bristol for many years, travelling to visit our grandmother and Auntie Eileen.

London was kind to me, offering rich and varied experiences and new relationships. Eventually, after working for *Ramblers Association* and *Wings Travel Agency*, I embarked on a career in social work. On my 21st birthday came the joyful birth of my youngest brother Marco.

That is another story. London was calling us towards a different way of life.

The Life of James White

There is a fine photograph, in classic Victorian style, of my great grandfather, James White, taken in 1889. James is bearded, has sensitive features and stands with hand on hip behind his wife, Emily, who is seated with the baby, Emily Rose, on her lap. Their other three children, Mary Rose six years, Robert five and Agnes aged three are grouped around them. My grandfather, Robert, looks rebellious, having argued over the possession of a toy ship with Agnes, so that James removed the ship.

This photograph was so compelling that I researched the White family. A thread of family memory but few facts led me back to the forgotten story of James. My mother, Margaret White, recalled her own mother, Nina, remonstrating with Robert that someone should have told her that James died in the asylum. However, her Aunt Mary Rose was indignant when asked if James was mad, and refused to talk about him. A myth prevailed that James had developed religious mania.

The Whites originated from Wiveliscombe, Somerset, where they lived in a beautiful valley home for hundreds of years. Parish records took me back to ancestors Richard and Sisly (Cecily) White who married in 1655. The Whites were mainly carpenters and weavers who later became stone masons, building houses in Wiveliscombe. My grandmother linked them with the Collard family, so possibly some of them made furniture for the Collards.

Around 1840, with the advent of the railway, my three times great grandparents, David White and Eunice (née Yandle) left Wiveliscombe with their five children and settled in Mill Lane, Bedminster, Bristol.

Their son, John, born 6th April 1834 in Wiveliscombe, adapted the family carpentry skills to become a cooper, making wine barrels in Bristol. On 6th July 1856 he married Mary Ann Dyer, daughter of James, a sailor, at St John's, Bedminster. John and Mary became the parents of James White who was born 3rd July 1859 at 5 Clark Street, Stapleton, a brother for David.

Following the death of his father, James became a scholar at the Queen Elizabeth Hospital School when aged nearly nine. At this time his mother returned to the paternal grandparents' home in Mill Lane.

Eventually James was apprenticed to a compositor, possibly C.T. Jefferies of Redcliffe Way. He was involved in printing a large volume of hymns translated from the Greek Orthodox Church, which was passed on to me.

James married Emily Rose, aged nineteen, on 18th February 1882 at St John's, Bedminster. He was then twenty-two years old. Emily was the daughter of Hugh Henry Rose, a corkcutter and Sarah (née Harvey, daughter of George).

Following the family photograph, a son, Frank Laurence, was born in February 1890. Then tragedy came to the family, culminating in the committal of James to the Asylum. His mother, Mary Ann, 'Fell asleep 19th April 1889 aged fifty-nine' and was buried at Arno's Vale.

In September 1890, his little daughter, Emily Rose, nick-named Ivy, died of scarlet fever aged two. James, then employed as a shipping clerk, was 'in attendance'. The family was living at 9 Park Terrace, Bedminster.

The following May the family lost their baby son, Frank, at the age of fourteen months. He had suffered from tuberculosis for six months and eventually died of exhaustion. His mother Emily was present at his death. Meanwhile, James was again employed as a type compositor. The two little children were buried with their grandmother.

A seventy-two year old relative, Geoffrey French, the son of Emily's sister, Matilda, told me that before he was admitted to the asylum, James went to live with his sister-in-law Matilda and her husband Harry French at Priory Road, Knowle. Geoffrey recalled that James became violent prior to admission to hospital, around 1895, where apparently he remained until his death in 1899.

My mother Margaret subsequently obtained a death certificate for James which showed that he died of encephalitis at Bristol Lunatic Asylum, aged forty, on 30th December 1899.

A psychiatrist at Glenside Hospital advised us that encephalitis once occurred in epidemic form. Death could occur several years after the acute phase of illness from the severe effects of the disease on the brain. The disease also gave rise to difficulties in the patient's control of emotions. This led, as with James, to many people in the past having to be admitted to hospital. Happily, the condition is now virtually unknown and there has been no epidemic in Bristol since 1928.

Mental illness has always been difficult for families to deal with, more so in the past than now and it is sad that James died with that stigma, as it was then regarded, and his 'secret' was buried with him.

My grandfather, Robert, was sent to an orphanage run by nuns which I was unable to trace. When great Aunt Mary Rose died, two letters were found written by James on Sunday 22nd December 1895 addressed to 48 Queen's Road, Clifton when he was in the asylum. The first letter was to Mary Rose who was then twelve years old, the second to her sister Agnes, then aged nine.

My darling Rosie,

I was very pleased to hear such a good account of your singing from your mother when she came to see me last and I hope you will try your very best with your music lessons so that when you are older you may be able to pass the examination for the Royal College of Music... Not so much that you may put certain coveted initials after your name but that they are evidence of your thoroughness in your studies. I hope you will have a very happy Christmas and a prosperous New Year. Give your pretty mother a kiss for me and tell her that Wednesday I hope she will kindly remember me at church and I know that you will not forget to do so also.

Will you tell her that Thursday next, being Bank Holiday, visitors are permitted to come all day with the exception of the dinner hour. So if the weather is fine and dry perhaps you and her could come. She need not bring anything as I have plenty of tobacco and I will pay your train fare.

From your dear Dad,
James White

My dear Agnes,

As I was writing to Rosie I thought you would like a little note from me. I hope you are a very good little girl to your dear mother for you can never repay her for the care she has given to you during my long absence from you.

I hope to hear you are getting on well with your lessons at school and when your brother Bertie comes home, mind and give him a kiss from me. Santa Claus will not forget you Christmas Eve if you have been an obedient little girl to your darling mother.

Goodbye, and may you have a very Happy Christmas and do not forget to wish Aunt Tilly many very happy returns of the day when you see her on Tuesday next.

From your loving Dad,
James White

In March 1978, James's grave was finally located at Arno's Vale. It was completely covered by greenery and took staff two hours to find it. James was buried with his mother, Mary Ann, and two youngest children, Ivy and Laurie. His widow, Emily, re-married Henry Allen, a tailor, and was buried with Henry and other relatives.

James was the only family member to be buried without an epitaph, the inscription says, 'Also James White, died 30th December 1899 aged 40 years'. Seventy-nine years after his death we finally knew and understood some of the suffering experienced by James and his family.

A stone mason added our inscription to James's tombstone; an epitaph from a family grave in the cemetery of St Andrew's Church in Wiveliscombe:

'Love's Greatest Gift, Remembrance
The Family, 1978.'

The Rose

Some say love it is a river
That drowns the tender reed.
Some say love it is a razor
That leaves your soul to bleed.
Some say love, it is a hunger
In endless aching years,
I say love it is a flower
And you that sow the seed.
It is the heart afraid of breaking
That never learns to dance.
It is the dream afraid of waking,
That never takes the chance.
It is the one who won't be waking,
Who cannot seem to give,
And the soul afraid of dying
That never learns to live.
When the night has been too lonely
And the way has been too long,
When you think that love is only
For the lucky and the strong,
Just remember in the winter
Far beneath the bitter snows

Lies the seed that with the sun's love
In the spring becomes the rose.

Sung by Bette Midler
from the film *The Rose*.

Last message from Margaret Attard to her children, played
at her funeral in South London, 24.6.93.